My Favorite Color is
The Golden Hour

Eva Austin

My Favorite Color is The Golden Hour

A Favorite Color Novel

Paperback
ISBN: 979-8-9857474-7-8

Ebook
ISBN: 979-8-9857474-6-1

Published by Inevah Press
Edmond, Oklahoma
www.inevahpress.com

For my hubby

My favorite love story

1

Emma

"Emma. Where'd you go?"

"Out here." I spring back into action, wiping the table.

The door creaks, and the bell overhead dings. "Caught ya." Olivia steps onto the front porch. The laughter in her wide-set hazel eyes dances in the glow of strung lights. She reaches up to adjust the wild, messy bun atop her head.

I relax and toss the cloth onto the table next to a cluster of mini pumpkins, Coffee Connection's autumn centerpiece. "I thought you were Joanna."

"Figured, by the way you hustled back to work."

She lets the door close, and I rub my arms. The air has turned chilly since the sun went down. "What's up?"

"She's looking for you. Joanna. It's your turn to clean the bathroom."

I groan.

"And good luck. It's a mess after that pack of kids tramped through."

"Not again. This has been the longest shift."

She checks her watch. I'm not the only one who powered through a busy day at the espresso machine. "Almost there."

Sidling next to me, she cranes her neck. "So what is it you were staring at over there? Oh, I see. McDreamy." She bumps my shoulder. "He's here late today."

She knew perfectly well who caught my attention. At the half-built house next door, the carpenter's son, a guy about two years older than me, is facing this way, bent over his workspace. Superbly framed in the bright window of the otherwise dark construction site, he stretches a measuring tape across the kitchen cabinet he's building, giving us a nice view of muscled arms.

"Actually, I changed it. It's McDarcy now. Until further notice."

"McDarcy?"

"Darcy. As in McDreamy plus Mr. Darcy."

She wrinkles her nose.

"You know, from *Pride and Prejudice*. Lizzie Bennet's hero?"

She shrugs.

"The romance novel of all romance novels by Jane Austen? Seriously. I can't believe you haven't read it."

"We're not all aspiring teen writers devouring every book that comes along."

"Olivia, it's classic. You should read it."

"Maybe I will… eventually."

Her gaze strays back to McDarcy. She sighs too, and we gawk, listening to the leaves tumble across the sidewalk behind us.

What nice arms you have, sir.

He's the perfect inspiration for the contemporary romance novel I'm working on. He's tall, handsome, and has great hair. Did I mention the muscles?

This semester-long banishment may work out after all.

"So why don't you get over there and talk to him? You've been staring at him all week."

I pull a lock of my dark hair over my shoulder. "I can't yet. I need to make this the perfect meet-cute. Otherwise, I don't get my novel inspiration."

"Meet-cute?"

"It's the moment in a novel when the characters first bump into each other."

"Ah, so walking over there isn't going to cut it?"

"Nope."

"Wait. Didn't you already meet the guy?"

I pluck the cloth from the table and wipe a half-hearted circle over it. "Well. Sort of. But Joanna did all the talking, and I didn't catch his name. So it doesn't count. Besides, meeting as we take out the trash is not nearly cute enough."

"Ah. Of course."

It needs to be perfect. That's why I'm giving him a do-over. He doesn't know he's getting a do-over. But he'll get it right next time.

Olivia shifts next to me as a dark curl falls over McDarcy's eyes, and he sweeps it aside. He picks up a pencil and marks the surface before him.

Note to self: write a scene in which I run my fingers through that great hair.

He glances up, catching our stares, and grins in that overconfident way. *Yeah, girls stare at me all the time.*

And he even has dimples. Jackpot! Ideal for the hero of any novel.

Olivia and I offer a little wave, mirrors of each other, smiling like idiots. Smooth.

He goes back to measuring and marking. I stand a moment longer, the grin still stretched across my face.

"Earth to Emma. Time to get back to work." When I don't move, she waves before my face. "Joanna? The bathroom?"

"Oh, all right." I swat her hand away with the cloth and huff my way into the coffee shop, where Joanna, the owner, tells me what I already know.

As I make my way down the hall, my phone buzzes in my back pocket. I pause and pull it out, finding a notification from my new favorite app, the J. A. Day (or Jane Austen Daily). It delivers a quote or passage by my girl Jane at random times once every day.

I swipe it open and read.

I shall be miserable if I have not an excellent library. ~
Pride and Prejudice *by Jane Austen*

Too true, Miss Austen. That's why I have big plans for mine. As I pass by a shelf lining this back hallway, I tap the book spines on it.

Hello, friends.

Here, Joanna allows me to stock a collection of novels for a lending library. It's more tucked away than I'd like, but I'm working on an alternative.

The thought has me smiling, but my mood shifts as I wriggle into plastic gloves.

Five short months ago, I was graduating from high school, and big life changes were on the horizon. College! Finally! Things were going as planned.

But sometimes, plans get derailed.

They blow up in your face.

And so, I'm here. Banished by my mother for "moping around." Now I'm making coffee and cleaning toilets—not at the same time—for someone named Joanna.

So why did my parents send me to this tiny town in the middle of nowhere?

To get "clarity and focus."

Too bad Mom thinks this clarity and focus will come in the form of cleaning their rental houses while their property manager is on maternity leave. Super.

I scrub away at the toilet.

Did Lizzie Bennett ever have to clean the privy?

Not after she snagged her McDarcy. That's for sure.

5

A few minutes later, when I emerge from the spotless bathroom, Joanna slings her purse over her shoulder. "I need to head out, ladies. Don't forget to lock up."

I flip the bathroom light. "Okay. Good night."

When the back door closes, I stand on my toes and peek out the high hallway window. Nope. The carpenter's not visible from here.

I put the cleaning supplies away and wash my hands. Twice.

Our take-two meet-cute needs to be epic. After I got dumped over the summer, my nonexistent love life— and my novel—could use some excitement.

I scoot across the hall and peer into the cooler's glass door. It's running low on expensive berry-flavored sparkling water, so I pluck a few from the stock closet.

Am I crazy to think I can arrange a meet-cute? Probably.

Is it unrealistic to think I can turn the experience into a novel? Maybe.

Admittedly, this is not my usual style. I tend to consider myself more of a realist.

But for this fall—for the next three months—I'm sunshine. Happy, bubbly, extroverted, sometimes annoying sunshine.

It's exhausting, to be honest, but it's time for a new approach. I'm tired of going for the wrong guy. I need something different. *I* need to be different.

Over the last year, I've read so many romance novels heralding the grumpy-sunshine trope I'm ready to bleed golden light. I've done my homework for my book and for this real-world scenario.

Can I take what I've learned and gain inspiration for my next self-published novel?

We'll see.

After the novel-worthy meet-cute, I'll ask him if he'll take on my small building project. Because, obviously, we need a project to force us together.

I shut the cooler and head back to the front counter. Olivia is already closing the register. I grab a rag to give the counter one last wipe down, making sure not to disturb her over-the-top decorating skills. Honestly, the shop looks like autumn threw up on it. Not that I'm complaining... much. I love this time of year.

The door dings again, and I turn toward it, ready to send the latecomer away with a smile.

But not ready for the person who steps inside.

The rag halts in my hand, my heart rate ticks up a beat, and familiar dark eyes go wide.

2

Emma

I still, lips parted, and suck in a shallow breath.

Bryson Dumar.

I haven't seen this boy in three years.

And… it hasn't been long enough.

We were friends once.

Best friends.

But not anymore.

My mouth snaps into a thin line.

Now that I'm older and more mature, I should be able to put the resurfacing feelings behind me, but I can't. They simmer through my veins.

He pauses, clearly not prepared to see me either.

He's taller than I remember. About six feet now. (Practically short compared to McDarcy's six foot three.

Just saying.) He wears jeans and a white hoodie printed with a run club logo, and his light brown curls fall over his forehead.

He was always cute. Too bad, the slight awkwardness of his early teens didn't linger. Nope. He looks good. Annoyingly good.

"Emma." He finds his voice. "What are you doing here?"

I wave the rag. I don't smile. "Cleaning. Obviously."

I'm not a rude person. I'm quite nice. Polite, even. But... Bryson Dumar. Invading my space!

He lets out a nervous laugh. "Obviously. Is your family in town?"

So he wants to play it like that. Pretend nothing happened.

"Nope. Just me." I busy myself wiping the counter again.

He hesitates at the coffee bar across from me.

I scrub with the rag. "We're closed. So you can leave."

"Come on. Can I please order? I promised my mom a green tea if she beat me in a board game. And I could use a coffee too."

"Sorry. Should have come earlier."

He pulls a ten-dollar bill from his pocket. "I have cash. You can run it in the morning and keep the change."

I shrug and plant a sorry-not-sorry expression on my face. "Nope."

Olivia, who I forgot was here, slams the register closed. "Emma, we can figure something out." Then, to me, she hisses, "Sunshine trope? That's you, remember?"

Sunshine? The sun went down an hour ago.

Bryson's smile is gone, and a muscle flexes in his jaw.

I cross my arms. "We're closed."

Olivia nudges me out of the way. "Hey, sorry about my friend. She's not usually like this... though it seems you already know her. I can give you hot water and a tea bag, and I can make a pour-over coffee without dirtying the machine. Interested?"

He smirks my way. "Sounds great." While the traitor does his bidding, he drops his ten on the counter. "Sunshine? I'm not feeling those vibes. Not how I would describe you."

I straighten the sugar packets. "You don't even know me." Anymore.

Olivia sets a paper cup of hot water in front of Bryson. She peels open the green tea pouch and bobs the bag before sealing the plastic lid. "I'm Olivia, by the way. I'm sure Emma meant to introduce us."

"I don't think she did." He sits on a stool and wraps both hands around the cup. "I'm Bryson Dumar. Nice to meet you."

"You guys renting for the weekend?"

"No. My parents own a place out here, but we don't make it out often anymore."

Olivia turns to grind the beans. Usually, I love the smell, but Bryson's ruining it. "So you owe your mom a tea. What game did you lose?"

He hesitates like he doesn't want to answer. His lips quirk up. "Candy Land."

I raise a brow, and Olivia laughs. "Nice."

"We were playing with my nephew. He won, of course, the little cheat, but then my parents and I battled it out to see who would take second. It wasn't me." He lifts a shoulder.

Olivia motions for me to hand her a cone filter. "I loved that game when I was a kid."

I reach for a filter, and my sleeve brushes a set of paint swatches to the floor. After passing the filter over, I pick them up and stack them on the bar.

"What are those for?" Bryson nods toward them, still holding his mommy's cup like a warm lifeline.

I hold my coffee like that. Note to self: stop cuddling my coffee. No matter how much I like it.

I slide the swatches away from him. "None of your business."

Yes, I'm acting like a child. But the carryover feelings I have from the last time I saw him are real, and I can't help myself.

Olivia shoots me an are-you-serious look before pouring steaming water over fresh-ground coffee.

She drums her fingers as the water drips into the paper cup. "She's about to build one of those Little Free

Libraries in front of her grandma's house and is deciding what color to paint it."

Seriously, is there no gal code at all?

Before I can stop him, Bryson slides the squares before himself and shuffles them into a neat line. "These are all over the place. Dark-gray, blue, yellow, white."

"They all mesh with the colors on the front of the house," I defend myself.

Olivia grips her hip and leans on the bar. "She likes the yellow."

I scowl at her.

Bryson picks up the swatch. "Like her sunshiny disposition."

I pluck it from his fingers. "It's not some random yellow. If you'll notice, it's called 'rusted mustard.' It complements the blue front door. And it's not a sunshine color. It's more like fall leaves."

"I like it." He stacks the other swatches and slides them to me.

I start to say thanks but instead press my lips into a thin line. I don't care if he likes it.

He's watching me with those beautiful deep-brown eyes I remember so well. I don't want to remember them.

He looks away first and studies his hands as they wrap around the hot tea.

Movement catches my eye when I turn away. Next door, McDarcy carries a plank of wood over his shoulder. He threads it out the front door to his truck.

His sweaty T-shirt sticks to his back. Muscles flex under it.

Olivia sets the coffee and another lid in front of Bryson. He's watching me again, this time with a slight downturn to his lips.

Not this again. He has no business having an opinion about who I like or spend time with.

I smirk and grab my purse, sliding the ten in front of the register.

Olivia tidies up the coffee bar *again*, and we walk out together.

He salutes the tea in her direction. "Thanks for these, and it was nice to meet you."

"No problem. Good night."

His smile vanishes. "Emma," he says in a tone I don't much appreciate. Then he takes off down the sidewalk.

I lock the door. "Ugh."

As he disappears into the darkness, McDarcy's truck roars to life ahead of us. He speeds past, allowing a two-fingered wave. In unison, Olivia and I wave back. Can we please be cool for once?

Eye on the prize, Emma.

Bryson's weekend in Carlton Landing won't matter. He'll be headed home in no time.

Olivia chuckles. "He's cute. And funny."

"No, he's not."

She elbows me. "What's wrong with you? There must be a story there. Who is Bryson Dumar to you?"

Only my best friend who betrayed me and broke my heart.

But I'm so *not* getting into it tonight. It doesn't matter.

I tear my gaze from McDarcy's taillights. "Who is he? That, my friend, is McDoom."

Olivia rolls her eyes. "Seriously? What grade are you in?"

3

Bryson

Is she seriously still mad at me after all this time?

One phone call—and I'm still not convinced it was the wrong thing to do—and then... nothing. She blocked my number and went on with her life, never looking back. Not once. I didn't have the chance to apologize, get her side of the story, or give mine. Nothing.

Well, if she can still be mad, so can I.

I kick at the pebbles underfoot, both in frustration and because the heat is seeping through these paper cups. Then I take the back steps up through the screened-in porch two at a time and kick against the door.

"Who is it?" a childish voice calls from the other side.

"It's me. Hurry, I'm getting scalded."

Tyler opens the door, and I rush past him, cross the hardwood floor, and slide the cups on the kitchen island. I shove my schoolwork aside as he climbs onto a stool beside me.

"Did you get me anything?"

I ruffle my nephew's shaggy brown hair. "No. Remember, you get Uncle Bryson's homemade hot chocolate." And by homemade, I mean by Swiss Miss. I grab a packet from the pantry and hunt for a mug.

Things have moved around in the three years since we were here. Renters and property managers aren't particular about putting things away. What a jumbled mess.

Like my mood.

I find plastic cups with The Meeting House logo in the back of a cabinet. I remember these. I liked the blue one, and she always wanted purple. Back then, I was in the business of ensuring she got what she wanted and was happy and smiling. Three years ago, I was a fifteen-year-old without a care in the world. Well, I had one care. And her name was Emma. But then everything happened, Dad's startup took off, and we moved to Houston. My sister got to stay in Oklahoma with her baby and husband. But not me. I had to leave everything. Houston's too far for a weekend trip to Carlton Landing. So I haven't been back. And I never heard from Emma again. Not until now.

I shove the cups back in the cabinet and fill one of my sister's old mugs. The words *Lake Hair Don't Care* form a bright blue arch above an embossed anchor.

While I microwave the milk, Tyler's feet thump against the island as they swing under the stool. "Not too hot."

"I know, buddy. Where'd Nana and Papa go?"

"Papa said he had some work to do. Nana went to find Chutes and Ladders. I bet I can beat you in that too."

"We'll see about that." I sit next to him, steepling my fingers and resting my chin on them.

"What's wrong, Uncle Bryce?"

"Nothing. Well, actually… do you have any friends that are girls?"

"Yeah. Lots."

I nod. "Sometimes girls are complicated."

He copies me and steeples his fingers. "Aleah gets mad if I don't play with her."

"That happens."

"Found it." Mom pads down the stairs, shaking the box. When she rounds the corner, her smile brightens. "Oh, yay, my second-place green tea. I'm so glad they were still open."

"Well, they weren't. But I managed."

I rescue the milk from the microwave, pour the brown powder in, and stir. "You won't believe who I saw working in there."

Mom plops down next to Tyler. "Who?"

"Emma."

"Emma?"

"As in Emma Blackwell."

Her eyes go wide. "Oh. We haven't seen her for ages...." Great. Now, she's watching me. "So, how is she?"

Rude. Annoying.

"Fine."

I never told Mom the details. She knew we fought and had a rough time that last summer, but I never admitted Emma blocked my number. Mom probably thinks the two of us just drifted apart since we moved away and haven't returned until now.

She drops five mini marshmallows into Tyler's mug.

"Thanks." He blows across the top even though it's barely warm and then splashes the granite counter when he tries to take a drink.

I pluck a napkin from the holder.

"Well..." Mom slides the game box aside. "What's she doing here? Is her family in town?"

"I don't know."

"What do you mean you don't know? You just ran into your childhood best friend. Didn't you ask questions?"

"She wasn't up for a chat. Actually, it kinda felt like we were still in the middle of a fight."

"Oh, surely not. That was ages ago." She sips her tea. "Too bad you two didn't stay in touch. You were such good friends."

I wipe at the brown puddles but don't respond.

"You know, you guys could reconnect. That could be fun. Plus, if she won't take the first step to restoring your friendship, then you should. It's the right thing to do."

Only if she doesn't bite my head off first. "We'll see."

She unfolds the game board, and her eyes take on a gleam that might mean trouble. "Maybe you two can rekindle whatever was between you back then."

I nearly choke on my coffee. "Mom, we were just friends. There's nothing to rekindle."

Tyler wipes the hot chocolate from his lip with his shirtsleeve. "What does it mean to be just friends?"

I meet Mom's gaze. "It means we didn't like each other like that. We weren't dating. We were. Just. Friends."

"Whatever you say." She sets up the spinner, selects a player, and hands Tyler and then me one. But she won't let go when I try to take it. "How did she look?"

I leave her gripping my player and wipe the already clean counter again. "Fine."

"Fine?"

"Good. She looked good."

"Good?"

"Okay." I throw my hands up. "She's as pretty as she always was." Prettier, even.

"I knew it." She plunks my player onto the damp countertop. "She was always such a cute girl."

Believe me, I noticed.

19

Tyler plucks a marshmallow from his mug and pops it in his mouth. "Nana, sometimes girls are complicated."

Mom raises a brow, and I ruffle his hair again, chuckling. "You know, the little dude has a point."

4

Emma

The next morning, I pad across the hardwood floors to the gourmet coffee maker and sift through glorious bags of ground coffee. I'm in the mood for flavored, and today is a southern pecan kind of day. After smelling the beans, I get the coffee going and set up my laptop on the smooth granite bar top.

So how does a marathon high schooler who works part time at a coffee shop afford this posh house?

Well, I don't.

My parents own this house and three others in Carlton Landing. This tiny community, nestled next to Lake Eufaula, is a great place to visit and to own vacation rentals.

It also used to be one of my favorite destinations in the world. But that was *before*.

It's not what most people think of when I mention a small town. I would describe it as more of a seasonal place—like a beach town in Florida. In fact, the same urban planner who designed Seaside, Florida, laid out Carlton Landing... smack-dab in the middle of nowhere Oklahoma. Crazy, right?

The house I'm staying in—one we call The Blue Moon—is a tiny two-bedroom two-bath right on the boardwalk. It took some convincing, but Mom agreed to let me stay here rather than in Mema's house since it was vacant. I love my mema, but I was supposed to go off to college like all my friends and be on my own by now. Staying here lets me experience some of that, even if Mema lives a five-minute walk away.

I jump as boots pound up the front steps but smile when a UPS worker drops two parcels on the porch swing and rushes away. I scramble outside into the crisp morning air, plop down beside them, then rip the first one open.

"Congratulations on your Little Free Library! Enclosed, find your charter sign."

I lift the small metal sign from its wrappings and read my library number engraved on it.

It's happening!

I open the other package and slide two paperbacks from it: a YA rom-com and a fall-themed sweet romance.

This is why I have to play barista while working for my parents. I love to buy books—hardback, paperback, ebook, audiobook—it doesn't matter. I ask for them for Christmas, birthdays, or just because. I brought all my books to Carlton Landing, and I have a lovely library going, if I do say so myself. Once I read these, they'll be considered for my Little Free Library. I'll curate the perfect selection.

I lean back, pulling my fluffy robe tighter around my shoulders, and take in the lovely Saturday morning.

Laughter carries on a burst of cool Oklahoma wind, and my hair whips across my face. I brush it away as elementary-age kids pound down the boardwalk on bright scooters. They're as loud as a herd of elephants, but I don't mind. And neither does anyone else. The weekenders' kids always get early starts.

An army of rust-colored leaves rush after them, and I shiver, gathering my things. On my way in, I straighten a bouquet of fake flowers in a flowerpot I display on the porch.

I *planted* daisies to add some color. They don't precisely match the season, but they're bright and cheery. Every time I leave the house, they remind me to present my sunshine persona to the world.

Back inside, I place my mail on the stylish coffee table next to my beloved camera and the blueprints for the Little Free Library. I'm waiting for the ideal opportunity to ask McDarcy to build it—or at least help me. Or watch me. I mean, whatever. I'm capable of building this on my own. It's not complicated for someone who knows how to use a drill—not that I've ever used one—but it's right up McDarcy's alley. Too bad he doesn't work on the weekends.

I'm on the Coffee Connection schedule tonight but off Sunday and Monday. I'll work on that meet-cute soon.

For now, it's time to focus. First, I'll post a few of my latest fall photos on my photography Instagram account, and then I'll lock in. Those two thousand words aren't going to write themselves. I may fail my one online class, but those words will make it into my laptop.

***

Like me, Bryson and his family attend the local community church on Sunday. I manage to avoid him, but his mother hustles my way and pulls me into a fierce hug.

"I was so glad when Bryson told me he'd run into you. Said you were just as pretty as ever." She pats me on the cheek. "And you sure are."

I don't quite know what to say. "Um… thank you. That's sweet of you."

Bryson thinks I'm pretty?

We chat about Carlton Landing and life until she realizes her family has left the sanctuary to make the short walk to Mama Tig's for lunch.

"Would you care to join us?"

"Oh. No thank you." I wave her off. "I'm heading to the house for lunch."

She squeezes my arm. "Well, it's a shame you and Bryson didn't have the opportunity to stay close after our last summer here."

Clearly, she doesn't know the full extent of her son's treachery.

"Yeah. Shame."

"Well, tell your parents I said hello. And thanks for the hot tea last night."

I stride the other way up the boardwalk. Well, I was planning to hit Mama Tig's pizza for lunch. But I'm not going there now.

So I make a peanut butter and jelly sandwich and curl up to write on the porch swing with a blanket, my notebook, and my laptop. I'm deep in thought when my phone vibrates with a text. I could leave it unread, but I'd better take a look.

Mom: Hey, honey. Just checking in. I hear the annual fall festival is coming up. You should help with that. I bet they'll need some artistic people on board. Doesn't that sound fun?!

That does sound like something I'd like. I could help with face painting or whatever.

Me: Yeah, cool. I'll look into it.

Mom: Oh, good. Because I already told them you'd help. Someone named Cole is in charge of volunteers. The first meeting is Monday evening at 6:00.

Seriously?

Me: Mom, you have to ask me before you volunteer me for stuff.

Mom: Oh, I knew it was right up your alley. Anyway, I'm mainly texting to inform you we may have a renter for The Blue Moon. It's not set in stone, but the Thomases are contemplating an extended trip sometime in the next month. You may need to move out. I'll keep you posted.

That's just awesome. My life is lived at my mother's whim. Emma, move here. Emma, clean this. Emma, move again. Emma, volunteer for this.

The fall festival sounds fun, but still.

I don't give her more than a thumbs-up emoji and then lean my head back against the swing.

Could something please go my way?

My phone buzzes, and I read my daily quote from the J. A. Day.

Angry people are not always wise. ~ Pride and Prejudice *by Jane Austen*

Hmm. Good thing I'm the sunshine character.

Two minutes later, McDarcy's truck rumbles past—strange for a Sunday. What's he doing?

I could find out.

Besides, my meet-cute plans don't need to change just because my mother is overbearing or Bryson is in town.

Maybe this is my moment.

I slam my computer closed and hustle to find my shoes.

The café will be the perfect place to finish today's writing session.

5

Emma

When I walk by the house McDarcy's been working in, he's nowhere to be seen. I cross to the café and push the door open with a ding. "It's me."

Olivia emerges from the storeroom. "Oh, good. Someone who can make their own coffee." She's piled her hair in its usual messy updo. Colorful feather earrings dangle almost to her shoulders, brushing against the exposed skin where her bright sweater's wide neckline swoops off one shoulder.

I drop my camera bag and blueprints on the coffee bar and nudge aside an assortment of plastic fall leaves. "Just as well. You don't make it right anyway."

She makes a disgusted sound but doesn't offer to make my drink as she refills the sugar packets.

Keeping an eye on the house next door, I grab a mug and brew up a pumpkin spice latte and a plan of attack. And by attack, I, of course, mean meet-cute.

I form a perfect leaf design on the coffee's frothy surface, savoring the spicy smell, and then sit at the coffee bar.

I take a sip. Exquisite. "Did you see McDarcy go inside next door?" He never works on Sunday, so I have no idea what he's doing or how long he'll stay.

"No. And, here, I thought you came to see me."

"I mean, of course, I came to see you."

"Sure. Sure. So what are you up to? You usually write at home on Sunday."

"I saw him drive by. And I'm ready for this meet-cute."

She leans her elbows on the bar and fights a smile. "Ah. So what's the plan?"

"You can laugh if you want. I'm fully aware of my idiocy."

"At least you're aware of it. That's the first step."

"I'm tired of waiting around for our opportunity to bump into each other. It's time to make it happen."

"I love the motivation, but why don't you just go over there and talk to him? You even have a reason." She indicates the blueprints.

"That's not cute enough. How would I write that into my novel?"

"Real life is not always like a novel. Sometimes it's messy or boring, and you might end up meeting Mr. Right somewhere equally as boring."

"Really? Like where?"

"I don't know. Like waiting in line for the bathroom or something."

I sip my latte. "Let's hope it doesn't come to that."

"Could be worse. You know, I bet they're almost done building those cabinets. One of these days, you'll show up, and he'll have moved on to another building site."

Maybe he's cleaning up to leave now.

Right. The pressure is on. "And on that happy note, I'm moving to sit by the window so I can see his front porch."

I plug in my laptop, pull my notebook from my bag, and settle in to pretend to write. No way am I focusing right now.

The guy next door is not my usual type. But since I usually go for the wrong guy, I'm trying something new.

Finally, *finally*, the door swings open, and he steps out onto the porch. He stretches, giving an exquisite view of his muscular torso, and then shuffles down the front steps.

What if he's leaving for good? I should at least find out if they're finished.

I surge to my feet.

"Olivia, I'll be right back. Watch my stuff."

"Okay." She calls from the storeroom.

I burst through the front door and nearly knock another customer off their feet.

Wouldn't you know? It's Bryson Dumar. Great.

He reels. "Whoa. In a hurry?"

"No," I lie.

Another guy about our age stands behind him.

I need to get them inside. Now.

I swing the door open for them. "Olivia will help you at the counter."

Bryson's brows pinch together. But he takes the door, and they step inside.

I rush down the wooden front steps onto the sidewalk, but McDarcy has disappeared. I look both ways. Where'd he go? I stroll in front of the house and peer into the open doorway, taking a tentative step toward the porch. No movement inside. He must be coming back.

I fight the urge to call, "McDarcy!" But that's not even his name.

This is Bryson's fault. I squeeze my fist into a ball.

Thwack. An earsplitting sound cracks behind me.

I yelp and whip around.

McDarcy freezes, his eyes wide as he steps onto the unkempt grass… directly from a bright-green porta potty.

You've got to be kidding. The sound must've been the door snapping shut behind him.

"You okay?" he asks.

I put a hand on my chest. "Yeah, um, I'm good."

31

"You sure?"

I nod stupidly. Find more words!

But… a porta potty!

I clear my throat. "I'm fine. The door startled me."

"Oh. Sorry."

We stand there for another moment.

"Did you—need something?"

Right. I'm standing on his building site, so there's no backing out. Might as well get on with it. "Actually, I was looking for you." I reach into my pocket. Nothing. I try the other one. Seriously? I left it in the café? This might be good. "I left the blueprints inside, but I was wondering if you were interested in building a Little Free Library for me."

He lifts a brow.

"I'll pay you, of course," I rush on. "I could help too."

"What's a Little Free Library?"

"Oh, it's a lending library. My grandma and I are putting one in at her house. She's the official steward. The actual library will look a lot like an oversized birdhouse, but I want ours to look like a mini Carlton Landing house. With a porch and everything. Maybe white trim, a metal roof, and shutters on each side of the doors." I stop talking. I'm rambling and using way too many arm gestures.

"You want me to build you a birdhouse?"

"No, no, it's a library. There's a website. You can also look at examples on Instagram. I could show you." I step toward the café. "I have the blueprints in Coffee Connection if you want to come in."

He doesn't budge. He just stands there squinting at me with those gorgeous blue eyes.

Eventually, he tilts his head toward the house he's been working out of for the last month. "I need to get going. I'm only here to pick up a few things. Sorry." He walks back up the porch steps.

"Oh, no worries. If you ever want to look at the blueprints, I'll be next door."

He makes his way up, then pauses at the top. "Do you have a building permit? And permission from the homeowner association?"

"A permit? For something so small?"

"My dad and I want to stay in good standing with the city. Lots of work here. I won't build anything without permission. They're pretty strict." He shrugs and then disappears into the house.

Well, that was awesome.

But... he didn't exactly say no. And he didn't say he wouldn't be back next week.

I drag myself back to the café.

"It's like I can see the future," Olivia blurts the moment I'm inside. "You did meet him in front of a bathroom! Only worse, a porta potty."

Olivia, Bryson, and the newcomer crowd my vacated table. Bryson holds my library plans where he sits in front of my laptop.

I snatch the blueprints from his fingers.

He smiles. "Who's McDarcy?"

6

Bryson

Oh, that struck a nerve.

I'm practically melting under Emma's fiery glare.

She's cute when she's mad.

Not that I noticed.

Her long brown hair flows in waves over her shoulders. Now, she shoves it back before slamming her laptop closed. She sends Olivia her best what-did-you-tell-him look. Cole, my innocent bystander friend, shifts in his seat.

Olivia chews the inside of her cheek, trying not to laugh. "I didn't tell them anything. Well, only that you're a romance author... and you plucked up the courage to ask the guy next door to build your library."

Hmm. Interesting. *McDarcy.* Is that what they call the carpenter?

I put both hands up. "I read the name on your screen. Is he your character?"

"You read my manuscript?"

"No, of course not. The name jumped out at me."

Some of the tension leaves her shoulders. "No. That's not his name. It's just filler for now. And why are you at my table?"

Olivia drums sharp violet fingernails on the table. "As you know, it's the best place to people watch."

Emma scoffs and sits in the fourth chair, turning toward Cole. "Sorry. Didn't mean to be rude. I'm Emma."

"Cole," he says.

Olivia smooths one of her feathered earrings. "Cole was around some this summer. We played bocce ball once. I believe I won."

"Not a chance." He pushes his dark-rimmed eyeglasses up his nose.

She gazes at him sweetly. "Well, it was so long ago, so who can say for sure?"

He laughs and flips his dark blond hair out of his eyes. "I can. I annihilated you."

"Oh, I believe you." Emma picks at the stitching of her cream-colored sweater. "She's not that good."

"Whatever." After pretending offense, Olivia nods toward the window and pushes back from the table. "So he said no to building the library?"

Emma pulls a lock of dark hair over her shoulder and threads the strands between her fingers in a way that feels way too familiar. "Not exactly. We'll see."

Olivia shrugs. "You guys want drinks?"

"That'd be great," I say. "I'll take a decaf latte to go."

Emma rolls her green-eyed gaze to the ceiling as if a decaf beverage is a huge disappointment. What's her deal?

Cole stands. "Americano for me. Can I help?"

"Sure." They continue to argue about the bocce ball game all the way to the coffee bar, leaving Emma and me to endure undiluted awkwardness at the table.

I used to think that, if we ever found ourselves in the same vicinity again, we might get past what happened and be friends. Judging by our recent interactions, though, that was a childish dream. Well, if she can't grow up, then the least I can do is annoy her. It shouldn't take much. "What's your book about?"

She busies herself by stacking the blueprints. She doesn't want to answer. Or talk to me at all.

I smile pleasantly.

She grits her teeth. "It's a romance. Contemporary with Jane Austen vibes."

"Ah. So that's where McDarcy comes from?"

She raises a brow. "You know *Pride and Prejudice*? What? Did you watch the movie with your girlfriend?"

"No. With my sister. So, McDarcy?"

"Yeah, that's where it comes from. Well, actually, it's a mix of McDreamy and Darcy if we're getting technical."

"Of course."

She smirks. "So why are you sitting in my seat?"

I smirk back and slide into the chair Cole was in. "Well, Olivia seemed interested in observing your interaction with the giant next door." I pick up the blueprints. Will she snatch them back? Huh. She doesn't. "So, do you think he'll do it? Help you with this?"

She taps her pen on the table. "I'm honestly not sure. All he said was that I might have to get a building permit."

"Surely you don't have to have one for that." He pauses. "But you should run it by the homeowner association."

"He suggested that as well."

"Well, there you go. The guy's smarter than he looks."

Now, she snatches the blueprints from my fingers and stacks them on her laptop. "Believe me, he looks just fine."

And there it is. That's what I figured. She's interested in him. I force the corner of my mouth to turn up. "Sure. If you like the tall, broody type with wild hair, a bad attitude, and a tendency to blow you off when talking to them. Oh, wait. You're a romance author. You *do* like that kind of guy. He's probably emotionally wounded too."

"We in the biz like to call it grumpy. Fitzwilliam Darcy was grumpy and quiet. He came off as rude, but he was just shy and introverted. And silently pining for Elizabeth. In my novel, her character is the sunshine heroine."

"Jane Austen's Elizabeth isn't always sunshiny."

"That's true." She finally holds my gaze. "She wouldn't put up with Darcy pursuing her after what he did. She wouldn't accept him."

I stare right back, pitching my voice low. "That's true. Until she did."

The air crackles between us, and her lips tilt into a frown. She's quiet until she says, "Anyway, Mema is the president of the homeowner association, so it shouldn't be difficult to get permission."

I shrug and lean back. "You know, I took a woodworking class sophomore year." I reach for the plans again. "This doesn't look hard."

She grabs them first and pulls them toward her. "I know. I'm sure I can handle it if I have to."

My unsaid offer hangs in the air until Olivia and Cole rejoin the table.

Olivia hands over my decaf. "What are you guys talking about?"

Emma thumbs her notebook. "We were just discussing the ins and outs of *Pride and Prejudice* and how Lizzie Bennet is a tough cookie."

Olivia cocks her head. "Bryson, you romantic. You've read *Pride and Prejudice*? She's always trying to get me to read it."

I remove the lid to cool my too-hot coffee. "It's a classic. I've read lots of classics."

Emma narrows her eyes. "You said you watched the movie."

"I did. You just assumed I didn't also read it."

She shifts forward over the table and pitches her voice into a false whisper. "And do you read other romance novels?"

"Not really. But you better believe I plan to have one by author Emma Blackwell downloaded on my phone before I go to sleep tonight."

She rears back. "Oh, please don't."

"It's happening."

Olivia grins. "In that case, you should know she writes under the name Emmie Blackwell."

Emma glares at her. "Traitor."

I cross my arms. "Noted. And do you write under any other pen names?"

"No," Emma blurts.

"Olivia, does she write under other pen names?"

"Not that I know of."

Emma tilts her chair back onto two legs and narrows her eyes. "What are you doing here anyway? It's Sunday night. Shouldn't you be heading back to Houston or wherever?"

Quick to change the subject. Hmm. Interesting.

Anticipating her reaction, I answer with a smirk. "We decided to stay for a month or two."

She almost spews pumpkin latte over the table as her chair falls forward onto four legs. "What?!"

7

Bryson

I drum my fingers on the table and raise a mocking brow. "I… said… we're staying a while."

I could get used to this Annoy-Emma plan.

"That's cool." Olivia happy dances in her seat as if she can make up for her friend's absolute horror. "It will be nice to have more people around in the offseason."

"Thanks. Should be fun. My parents were looking for a slower pace, and since we still have our house here, Carlton Landing was the clear choice. We'll be here at least until the end of the year."

Cole nods. "Us too. Our families work together, and it's been a wild few months. Even more travel than usual."

And it's true. Our parents have been working like crazy to sell their startup. Dad will still have to travel some, but I'm looking forward to staying put. And we even get to babysit my nephew for a couple of weeks, which is cool. Can't do that on the road.

Cole's family enjoyed their time here this summer so much they decided to come too. Carlton Landing is the perfect spot for a slowdown.

Granted, I didn't know I still had an enemy here.

"What about school?" Emma blurts, her voice rising. "Aren't you a senior?"

"We've been homeschooling for the last two semesters since we travel so much. We'll keep doing that."

Emma may only be three months older than me, but I'm a year behind her in school. Why isn't she off at college by now? She always talked about going.

Before I can ask about it, though, her eyes go wide, and the hand bringing her cup to her mouth pauses. "Wait, you still own the place on Lower Greenway? The same house?"

"Yeah. We've been renting it out all this time. Why? Do you still live on Lower Greenway?"

She turns away toward the window, clenching her jaw and crossing her arms. "No."

Really? She's this mad we'll be in the same town? Talk about holding a grudge. The things that went down between me and her and that pretty boy, Eric, happened over three years ago.

43

Get over it already. I don't remember her being so cold—she wasn't cold back then. She was sweet and fun and… beautiful.

Still is. Beautiful, that is.

She's prettier than ever but clearly still hates me.

Her gaze fixes on something out the window. Ah, the carpenter has emerged from the house next door. He's disgustingly sweaty, but Emma doesn't seem bothered.

Not that I care.

I'm glad he brushed her off. She deserves it.

Olivia tells us about the different things to do both here and in the neighboring town of Eufaula. Cole nods, hanging on her every word. He should take notes.

Emma threads strands of her hair through her fingers again… just like she used to. Memories I'd long forgotten engulf me. Sitting on my screened-in porch. Drinking too much Dr Pepper late at night. Tearing across the green on a mountain bike. Laughing at all the cheesy rom-coms she forced me to watch.

Then Eric came along, and the scene changed—the two of them deep in conversation. Them making plans without me. Their whispered exchanges during our movie nights. Then her shutting me out.

I glare out at the bright-green porta potty. Yeah, she deserves it.

After a few more minutes, Cole stands. "Well, I better go. I've already been roped into heading up a committee for the fall festival. Leader's meeting in thirty."

I sip from my paper cup. "Don't pretend you don't love it."

"Fine. I love it."

Olivia pushes back from the table as customers bound up the front steps. "How'd that happen? You just got here."

"Our rental is next door to Mr. Johnston, the event chair, and he asked if I wanted to. I figure it will look good on college applications."

"How great. I love the fall festival."

"I'm glad to hear you say that because I need some volunteers for my committee, and our first volunteer meeting is tomorrow night. Can I count you guys in?"

Olivia stands and heads to the espresso machine. "Sounds fun. I'm in."

Cole swings his gaze my way, and I raise both hands. "You already pressured me. I said I'd do it."

He checks his notepad. "Emma, your mom said you were in, right?"

She opens her mouth. Closes it. Her gaze cuts to me. "I don't think I have time for that."

I cross my arms. "Really? Too busy?"

She scowls. That's my cue to leave. I don't want to be left alone with this scorned beauty. She might eat me alive or lure me into a trap like some siren of Lake Eufaula.

I push the lid back onto my coffee cup as Cole turns away. "Well, let me know if you change your mind. We could use more people."

She reopens her laptop. "I will."

Shrugging on my jacket, I follow Cole to the door. He's almost through when Emma says, "Bye, Cole. Nice to meet you."

"Bye." He waves.

When I glance back, her smile falls away. "Bryson," she says, deadpan.

No smiles for me.

Not that I care.

"Emma." I use the same inflection.

Cole claps me on the shoulder as we descend the porch steps. "So... care to explain what's up with you and Emma?"

"It's nothing."

"Right. Nothing. I've never known anyone who didn't think you hung the moon."

I smirk. "That's not true."

"I'm serious. I mean, if looks could kill, you'd be dead."

That's for sure. "She's still holding a grudge over something during our summer before I moved to Houston."

We step off the sidewalk and cross, turning onto Lower Greenway. "What happened?"

"I told on her when she and some guy snuck off to Eufaula one night."

"Oooh. Snitch. So they got in trouble?"

"I assume so. But I'm not sure. We left the next day, and I never talked to her again." I run a hand through my hair. "We were best friends."

"Hey, maybe you can make amends." He grins. "No telling what might happen then." He wags his eyebrows and shoves his glasses higher on his nose.

I laugh, kicking at a rock. "Are you serious? She hates me. And she ghosted me. Who does that?" I shake out the tension in my neck. "Like I said, we were friends. And now we're not."

Not to mention, the experience made me question every friendship I've had with a girl since then.

"Nah, she doesn't hate you. She just needs you to grovel a bit."

"I'm not groveling for something that happened three years ago."

"Shame. Groveling for someone that pretty could be fun."

This statement irritates me for reasons I can't explain. Why should I care if Cole thinks she's pretty?

I'm just glad she's not working the fall festival with us. That will make it easy to avoid her.

We thread between my house and the neighbor's and pound up the back steps, through the screen porch, and to the back door. Mom has left the top half of the Dutch door open this evening.

As I turn the handle, Cole says, "Well, if you don't plan to ask her out, then maybe I will."

I whip my head around to meet his smug gaze.

An irritating smile cuts across his face. "That's what I thought."

Why is everyone so annoying today?

I go inside and kick the door closed before he can come in.

"You know, slamming the door on someone has less effect when it's just half a door." He chuckles like he's just caught someone in a lie.

But he hasn't. Has he?

8

Emma

On Monday morning, I tuck into writing and brainstorming. One of my favorite writing memes says something like, "Being an author is 20 percent writing and 80 percent staring into the distance." And it's true. But I've been doing the staring and thinking part too much lately.

Also, my mind keeps drifting to Bryson and his judgy, albeit beautiful eyes. I don't have to help Cole with the fall festival if I don't want to. I mean, I did want to before I knew Bryson was doing it.

Now, I don't.

And I'm busy.

After lunch, I spend my afternoon cleaning porches. I haven't devoted as much time to my parents' rental properties as I should, so I grab my earbuds and sweep off my porch first, not forgetting to admire the sunshine-yellow fake daisies stuck in a flowerpot.

Bright and cheery. That's me. I put on my sunshine character as I take off down the boardwalk to Park Street.

I make the rounds, sweeping, shaking rugs, and watering plants. Once I've finished these chores, I hit the pavement again, singing along with the song blaring in my ears.

While in town, I also help Mema with odd jobs, so I head to her place.

She meets me at the door. "Hey, sweetie. I saw you coming. How are you?"

I step inside, and the hardwood floor creaks as it has for years, the soundtrack to every childhood Carlton Landing adventure.

She pulls me into a hug, and I lean into her, inhaling the scent of apples and cinnamon. "I'm good. Cleaning porches today, and yours is next."

"Aren't you a doll? I'd help, but Susan and I are running to the grocery store in Eufaula."

"That's okay. I can manage." I pluck a candy from the always-stocked coffee-table bowl and peel the wrapper away. "Did you know the Dumars moved in next door?"

"I do. I saw Barbara and Kevin this morning. They say they're staying a while." She eyes me over her glasses. "Must be nice to have your old friend back in town."

Not her too. I ball my hand into a fist. "Bryson and I were friends. Past tense. You know this." I toss the wrapper in the trash. "Not anymore."

"You mean to tell me you haven't forgiven that boy yet? It's been such a long time."

"Not long enough."

A car parks out front, and she tugs on my ponytail. "Well, Emma, that's something you should work on. Oh, I typed up your homeowner association permission form for the Little Free Library. It's on the counter. And I also picked up the supplies you mentioned at the hardware store. They're in a box on the porch."

I squeeze her. "Thanks, Mema."

"No problem. I'm excited for it to all come together." She checks her watch. "You'll be gone by the time I get back, so I'll see you at the festival meeting tonight."

"Oh, I'm not going."

Her eyebrows shoot up. "But I'm bringing autumn tea and apple tart. Your favorite. Why don't you want to help with the festival?"

"I'm so busy with the houses and the coffee shop and my book. Your baking smells amazing, though."

"Well, suit yourself. But I bet you'd enjoy it. I'll see you later and bring leftovers if there are any."

I wave her out and wind my way through the upstairs hallway to the bunk room where my sisters and I slept during our many Carlton Landing getaways.

This room is a child's dream. Not only are there four built-in bunks, but above that, up a ladder, and at the third level, there's a loft, a secret space for kids to meet for supersecret meetings. I haven't been up there in years.

I cross the room, throw open the double doors, and walk out onto the covered second-floor balcony. A sliver of lake peeks above the trees on the other side of Ridgeline Road.

I hum as I sweep the porch and dust the furniture. I use the broom to tackle a smattering of cobwebs on the white railing.

The occasional pedestrian meanders down the street, some offering a wave. I recognize most of them from my time in the café.

But my broom stills when a familiar figure rounds the corner up the street and heads this way. Bryson strolls toward his family's house, which is inconveniently situated next to this one.

I can't believe he's staying.

For three months.

Next door to Mema.

I slink back and sit on the love seat against the wall. I turn down the volume on the music blasting in my ears —though I don't know why because he can't hear it— and watch him through the railing slats, my mind drifting back to another time. A time when we got along. A time when we were friends.

I first came to Carlton Landing when I was eleven after my dad learned about it online. My parents just had to see it. I mean, how often do people start a whole new town?

So we packed up and drove the two and a half hours from Oklahoma City with a plan to stay three nights over spring break. We rented a cute two-bedroom house on the boardwalk, just a short walk to the beach.

We loved the small-town feel and ended up staying the week.

I met Bryson only hours after we arrived. We'd been swimming, and my little sister, Lucy, nine years old at the time, wasn't ready to leave. My parents stayed with her at the pool, and my older sister, Audrey, and I hopped on our bicycles with a promise to check back in thirty minutes. As we rolled along Park Street, a slew of kids raced by. We paused but couldn't quite figure out what game they played. By the time we'd circled Firefly Park, the kids were biking back in our direction. One of the boys, a kid about my age with shaggy light-brown hair, skidded to a stop next to us.

"You guys want to play?"

Audrey nodded, and I gripped my handlebars. "Okay. What do we do?"

"Follow me. I'm Bryson, by the way." He pedaled away, and we raced to catch up.

"There they are!" someone yelled from the front of the pack.

I craned my neck as two kids on foot threaded between houses.

It turns out we were playing a game called cat and mouse, and we were the cats out to catch the two mice. Mom and Dad let us stay out on our bicycles until twilight. I'd never had so much fun.

That night, after a late dinner, I ventured out onto the second-floor balcony of our rental house. I'd just laid out board game pieces on the wicker coffee table when voices drifted over from the balcony next door.

It was the boy who asked us to join their game!

A woman told him she couldn't play cards tonight but promised to play tomorrow. She went inside, and the boy half-heartedly shuffled his deck.

I rested my elbows on the white railing facing his house. "Hey, Brandon. What'cha doin'?"

He spun around, squinting into the darkness. "Who's asking? And... it's Bryson."

My cheeks heated as he walked closer. "Sorry. It's me. Emma. Remember? I didn't know you were next door."

He leaned over his railing. "I didn't know you were next door." He smiled and cocked his head to the side. "Were you spying on me?"

I laughed. "No. Not much."

He nodded toward my game. "Are you playing by yourself?"

"No, my sisters are coming."

His shoulders drooped.

"But you could join us. Want to come over?"

His deep-brown eyes lit up. "Yeah. Let me ask my mom."

"Okay. I'll meet you downstairs."

And that was that. The next day, us kids had more adventures, and that night, Bryson's family had ours over for dinner. By the end of the week, Mom and Dad had made an offer on the house.

Every summer after that—and many a holiday—was spent in Carlton Landing. Other friends came and went, but Bryson and I were inseparable—the best of friends.

Now, as I peek over the balcony railing, an eighteen-year-old version of that former friend jogs up the front steps of the house next door.

My phone tells me it's time for the Jane Austen Daily, so I swipe it onto my screen.

I cannot fix on the hour, on the spot, or the look or the words, which laid the foundation. It is too long ago. I was in the middle before I knew I had begun. ~ Pride and Prejudice *by Jane Austen*

It was too long ago. Too many memories. Too much history. Some good. And… some bad.

That last summer, before Mr. Dumar moved their family to Houston, we hung out on this very porch night after night. The world slipped by, and everything was about to change. They wouldn't be able to spend entire summers in Carlton Landing anymore. We were fifteen years old, heading into our freshmen and sophomore years of high school. Audrey, Bryson, me, and other neighborhood kids still played our games: cat and mouse, volleyball, bocce ball. But more and more, we were content to sit and talk or play board games or collectively stare at our phones while lounging around.

Then, around the start of July, a new boy blew into town. Outgoing, fun, and cute, he was the kind of boy everyone thought was cool, even Bryson at first. Eric Tucker always came up with exciting adventures.

But from Eric, I learned that not all adventures are worth the cost. And all the trouble I got into could have been avoided if it hadn't been for him... and Bryson Dumar.

9

Emma

I grip the broom tighter as a song Bryson and I used
to listen to starts up in my ears. The two of us listened
to it on repeat the summer we turned thirteen.

I skip it.

No time for that. I have cleaning to do.

Half an hour later, I stomp down the stairs, singing
along to a song that has nothing to do with Bryson, and
get to work on the downstairs porch.

As I finish up, my phone vibrates in my pocket. My
sister's name flashes on my screen.

Audrey: I'm spending the afternoon with Mom. She
wanted me to ask how the houses are looking.

Me: Why didn't she ask me?

Audrey: We're in line at Target, and I wouldn't let her voice text. You know how she is.

I send a laughing emoji. Mom loves to text but doesn't like to type it out. It's voice text or nothing with her. And because of her residual East Texas accent, Siri doesn't always understand her. This only makes her louder.

Audrey: Now she's giving me a dirty look.

I snap a selfie of myself in front of the house, ensuring the broom is visible.

Me: It's coming along.

Audrey: Mom says nice work. Now, she wants to know how your online class is going.

Honestly, not well. I'm way out of my league, taking a virtual programming class.

Me: It's fine. Also coming along.

Audrey: Now she's asking what time the festival meeting is tonight.

Me: I'm not going.

Audrey: She says, yes, you are.

Me: Nope. What are you doing in Oklahoma City?

There's a pause, and Audrey must be telling Mom to let it rest.

Audrey is a sophomore at Oklahoma Christian University, so it's strange for her to be home hanging out with Mom on a Monday afternoon. Did she skip class?

Audrey: Just needed a change of scenery. *Frowny face*

What? I close the texting app and call her.

She answers on the first ring. "Hey." Her voice sounds tired.

"What's up? Are you okay?"

"Emma. I'm in line at the store, remember."

"Hi, Emma," Mom says overloud.

"Hey, Mom. Audrey?"

"Nothing, really. Let me call you back when we get in the car."

"Fine. Call me back."

We hang up, and I slump down onto the front steps.

"Trouble in paradise?" a disembodied voice calls from next door.

I whip around as Bryson's head peeks over the porch railing. He's lounging on a hanging swing.

Just great. "How long have you been lying there?"

"A while. Nice singing, by the way. I'd forgotten you have an annoyingly decent voice."

I frown. "Have you also forgotten I don't like to sing in front of people?"

He smirks. "You know, that did come back to me."

I huff and gather my supplies.

He sits up. "I thought you didn't live here anymore."

"I don't. Mema does."

"Year-round?"

"Yeah, she moved in a year ago since we weren't coming as often. She loves it here."

He nods and seems about to say something else when his mom calls his name from inside.

"Out here."

"The screen door is stuck again," she yells through the window.

I cock my head and pitch my voice low. "*The* screen door?"

He chuckles. "I never told her you're the one who knocked it off the track."

"I wasn't the only one playing volleyball in the house."

For a moment, his smile distracts me, but then I remember why we're not friends.

He shakes his head at my abrupt frown. "Well. Off to the rescue. See you later. Or not."

My phone vibrates again, and I turn away to answer it. "Hey. All checked out?" I'm on speakerphone in Mom's car.

"Yeah. Finally. Mom had coupons, and the self-checkout nearly did us in. It was touch and go there for a while. I'm sure the attendant will tell his family about us around the dinner table tonight."

"Obviously."

Mom lets out an exasperated sound.

"Is Lucy with you?" I ask. Our little sis is starting her high school sophomore year.

"No, she's at school."

"Oh, right. Which is where you should be. And that brings me back to my original question. What are you doing there? Is everything okay?"

Audrey sighs. "Seriously, it's nothing. I'm just fed up with boys. As usual."

"Did something happen?"

"Not really. A guy in my speech class asked me out, but it turned out to be a group thing. I felt like an idiot."

"Oh no. Well, maybe he wanted to hang out in a low-pressure situation and get to know you."

"Yeah, maybe. We'll see."

"She heard Drew is dating someone," Mom says.

Ah, there it is. The real reason Audrey's upset. I nearly groan. She's been pining for him, her longtime crush, since they met years ago.

"Ah, sorry, Aud." I'm not that sorry. It's time to move on, but I hold that thought in. "You're going to meet someone great."

"Yeah, I know. It's fine. I just needed to get away for the day. It's no big deal."

Bryson's front door creaks open, and his head peeks around it. "Hey, Emma. Don't leave. Mom wants to give you some pumpkin muffins. She's putting them in a baggie."

I nod, hoping Mom and Audrey didn't hear, but the questions have already started.

"Who was that?"

"Someone you're seeing?"

"Is he nice?"

"Is he cute?"

"You already know his mom?"

Leave it to them to jump to conclusions. They talk over each other so quickly I can't tell who's asking what.

"It's no one. I have to go."

"What? No. I told you my story."

They'll read too much into this. Audrey always thought Bryson and I would eventually date. "It's Bryson Dumar. I wasn't even sure their family still owned the house next door until this week."

The talking and squealing following this statement are more than my eardrums can take. I hold the phone away. Bryson walks back out and perches on the railing across from me. He raises an eyebrow.

I shrug and put the phone back to my ear—time to end the call. "Listen, guys. He's back. I've got to go."

"Put us on speakerphone," Mom practically yells. Audrey must be driving because Mom does this when she's in the passenger seat and knows the microphone is on the other side of the car.

"Absolutely not." Though, Bryson likely hears them anyway.

"Is he going to the fall festival meeting? Emma, you need to go."

Audrey comes to my defense. "Mom, she doesn't want to."

"Seriously, gotta go, guys."

"Is he still cute?" Mom yells.

"Oh, good question," says Audrey.

I nearly drop my phone in my haste to hang up. Then I catch his smug grin.

"So your mom thought I was cute? And Audrey? Or was that Lucy?"

I groan. "Definitely not. And that was Audrey, not that it's your business."

He's still grinning as he stretches across the space between us. "Quick, take these before I smell them."

Oh, right. He doesn't like pumpkin flavor.

I start to ignore him and refuse the gift. But it would be rude to his mom, and I can't force myself to say no. Yummy. I snatch the muffins and then head down the steps.

I roll my eyes as he waves, giving me a smirk too cute for my liking. "So you are going to the meeting."

"Not a chance."

Besides, how can you trust anyone who doesn't like pumpkin muffins?

10

Emma

On my walk home, my phone vibrates with call after call. Finally, I answer and can't utter a greeting before Mom says, "I can't believe she hung up on us."

"Emma? You there?"

"I'm here. Aren't you home yet?"

"We're sitting in the driveway waiting for you to answer. Start talking. Why are you hanging out with your yummy nemesis, Bryson Dumar?"

"First of all, he's not yummy. I call him McDoom now, and I would appreciate it if you'd do the same. Second, I'm not hanging out with him. He lives next door to Mema and came out uninvited."

"But what about the muffins?"

Mom mutters, "I'm not calling him that."

"They were from his mom. Not him."

"Maybe he wants to reconnect."

"I don't want to reconnect."

"Why not?" Mom asks. "You guys were such good friends. I always thought he'd make a great catch for some lucky girl."

"Yes," Audrey says. "And obviously, we all thought it would be you."

Give me patience. "Guys, need I remind you about our past? I don't like him. I don't trust him. Plus, even if that wasn't an issue, I'm going off to college next semester."

"You can move past all that. I just love their family."

What if Mom starts playing matchmaker? Yikes. "I have a crush on a carpenter here in town, so you can forget it with McDoom."

"That poor boy. Don't call him that."

"Mom, I saw Mrs. Dumar on Sunday, and she asked about you."

"Oh, I need to give her a call."

Now I've done it. What's wrong with me? "Mom, remember, I like someone else."

"Yeah, yeah, I've got it."

"Tell me about the carpenter," Audrey says.

"Barbara, hey, it's Linda Blackwell." I hear Mom say, not to me.

"My word, did she call Mrs. Dumar *right now*?"

"It seems so."

"Ugh. I'll tell you about the carpenter during your fall break visit. He's going to spark some inspiration for my latest Austen-inspired rom-com. He just doesn't know it yet."

She laughs. "Can't wait to see him… and read the book." There's a pause, the ignition dies, and I'm not on speakerphone anymore. "Well, at least answer Mom's question about Bryson while she's not listening." Her voice drops to a whisper. "Is he still cute?"

"Not you too?"

"Well?"

"Of course, he's still cute. You don't just stop being cute after three years."

"So you do think he's cute?"

"Audrey, focus. The carpenter!"

"Right. The carpenter. Fall break. On it. I can help you."

"No. No. I'm fine. You and I will hang out and have a good time—sister bonding and all that."

"What's his name? Can I Google him?"

Incredible. "No. You may not. Mostly because I don't know his name."

"You… don't know his name?"

"I'm working on it."

"Well, you have to start somewhere. And after that bad breakup, I'm glad you're into someone new."

Mom's voice hovers nearer. She must be pacing. "Oh, she always goes for the wrong guy."

"Is she talking about me?"

"I doubt it. Who knows."

I frown, not comforted in the least. "Please try to get her off the phone."

Audrey's keys jingle in the background. "Will do. Oh, I just remembered we have frozen things in the back, and it looks like Mom is too busy to help. I better get them inside."

"Okay," I say at a loss. "Talk to you later."

We hang up.

What have I done?

***

A half-hour later, I push through the coffee shop's door for some much-needed caffeine with my official homeowner association letter tucked in my laptop bag. Now, I just need to wait for McDarcy to leave for the day and catch him on his way out.

I drop my bag on the coffee bar while Olivia stacks mugs in the industrial dishwasher. She blows a bubble from her palm toward me. "I've got news about your guy next door."

I raise a brow. "Oh?"

"His dad came in to grab a couple of sandwiches, and I asked how it was coming next door. I mean, it is kind of loud for our guests. He said all the cabinetry should be done within the week."

I slump against the bar. "Oh no."

"Yep. As we feared, the infamous McDarcy will be moving on. But hey, he might not go far. There's a ton of work around here."

"This is terrible. I only have days to convince him to build the library."

She shrugs. "Like I said, he might not go far."

My lips pull down at the corners. Then Joanna comes in the back door, and Olivia saunters off to greet her and switch out their shift.

I meander to my table near the window and set up my laptop, watching the porch next door.

When Olivia finishes clocking out, she slings her purse over her shoulder. "You sure you don't want to tag along to the volunteer meeting? It might be fun."

"No, I'm good." I've had enough of Bryson Dumar today.

She pitches her voice low. "Right. You have stalking to do."

"That's not what I'm doing! I want to hire him for a job."

"Uh-huh."

"Okay, maybe I'm stalking him"—I pinch my fingers together—"a little bit."

"There ya go. The first step is admitting it."

"Get outta here." I flick my hand toward the door, and she flips her hair over her shoulder.

"Fine. I'm early but might head over and see if Cole needs help. See ya later."

I settle into writing until my phone buzzes about fifteen minutes later.

Olivia: You might as well go home. He's not next door. He's here.

Me: Who?! McDarcy?

Olivia: yeah

You've got to be kidding.

Me: Why's he there?

Olivia: He and his dad are building a stage of some sort for the festival. They're the "building committee." So, good news. He'll be around for a while longer.

McDarcy is at the meeting?

If I go too, I could offer to help with the stage, and then, in exchange, he could help with the library.

This would be a prime opportunity in a romance novel to throw the lovebirds together and force them to spend time together.

It's perfect.

My smile slips as I tap my nails on the table. But Bryson will be there, and I'm in avoidance mode.

I shake my head and slam my laptop closed.

I can't let that stop me.

Me: Save me a seat. I'm coming.

11

Bryson

I arrive at The Meeting House early. Locals having dinner watch football on the big-screen TV in the corner. I wander to the side room reserved for the meeting.

Cole and Olivia are already bent over a clipboard, engaged in a quiet conversation.

Olivia giggles.

Hmm. What's going on there? They didn't even notice me walk in.

I step in their direction as they move to introduce themselves to two people across the room. I freeze. It's Emma's carpenter and an older man. My lips turn down. Did I just think of him as "Emma's carpenter"?

Gross.

I turn away, not wanting to get stuck in a conversation with *McDarcy*.

The door dings, and a familiar face lights up. "Bryson. What a pleasant surprise! I was so happy to run into your parents yesterday."

Mrs. Davis pulls me into a one-arm hug as she maneuvers a plastic container with the other hand and then steps back to look me over. "My, you've grown! Look at you! The last time I saw you, you were this tall." She holds up a hand around my chest area. "What a handsome young man you're becoming."

"Thank you, Mrs. Davis. How are you?"

"Oh, good. Good. I talked to your mom yesterday. I'm so glad you guys will be staying a while."

"Thanks. Me too. I've missed Carlton Landing."

Mrs. Davis, Emma's grandma, is our neighbor. I spent many a hot afternoon drinking lemonade on their upstairs porch.

With Emma.

I shove my hands in my hoodie pockets. "Are you here to volunteer for the festival?"

"Not this time. I'm here with refreshments"—she gives the container a shake—"and to see if any committees need anything from the homeowner association. I'm the president nowadays."

"That's cool."

"I tried to get Emma to volunteer, but for some reason, she backed out at the last minute."

It's me. I'm the reason.

And why does this bother me so much?

I check the time on my phone. "Where is everyone?"

Mrs. Davis tosses a bright-pink purse on a chair. The chairs have been arranged into a circle lining the wall. "Oh, they'll be here. We're on lake time, as I'm sure you remember. We'll get started in a bit, I imagine."

She meanders away to greet others.

Olivia and Cole notice I'm here, and we claim seats together near the exit.

The room slowly fills with people of all ages as six o'clock comes and goes.

"Emma!" Mrs. Davis says with a delighted smile. "What are you doing lurking in the dining room? You look like you're hiding. Come on in. I'm so glad you decided to come."

Emma?

Mrs. Davis maneuvers the girl into the room. She's on the verge of protesting when her gaze lands on the carpenters. Her mouth snaps shut.

Ah. Mystery solved. He's why she's here.

"Find a seat, honey." Mrs. Davis points my way where the only remaining empty chair rests at my side.

This should be fun.

Emma's eyes widen and then narrow. There's nothing for her to do but head my way if she doesn't want to seem rude in front of all these people.

I smirk at her as the festival chair, Eli Johnston, stands to bring this six-o'clock meeting to session seventeen minutes late. Emma ignores me and sits.

Close.

Her knee brushes mine, and she snatches it away. I don't bother scooting to make room. I enjoy her annoyance too much.

She bounces her foot and threads that hair through her fingers. A scent, one I remember well, something like coconut and tropical flowers, drifts my way, and I'm transported back to those long summer evenings.

Stop remembering.

Residual feelings—whether good or bad—are creeping up, and I so don't need them right now.

She stares forward, pretending Mr. Johnston has her full attention, but she's aware of me—just as I'm aware of her. Displeasure—or something like it—rolls off her in waves. My attention snaps to the front when I hear my name. Mr. Johnston has introduced Mrs. Davis.

"Many of you may recognize my granddaughter, Emma, and this is Bryson Dumar. His family is back in Carlton Landing for a time. These two were thick as thieves a few years ago. They were so good to include all the neighborhood kids. You remember, don't you, Bill?"

An older man wearing a fishing-themed T-shirt slaps his knee. "Sure do. My wife always imagined you two would end up together someday. Run off to college and life, and then come back here for the summers with your offspring."

Did he say offspring?

I cringe and peek at Emma.

Her foot pauses midbounce, and her cheeks flame a lovely pink. Her mouth slides half open, as if she needs to say something but doesn't know what.

The older generation chuckles, and Olivia presses her lips together.

Emma was always more prone to embarrassment than me. I force a laugh, and when she whips her icy gaze my way, I shrug.

Mrs. Davis swats at the air. "Oh, Bill, stop. You'll embarrass them."

Too late. Bill doesn't appear to care in the least.

Luckily, Mr. Johnston regains control of the meeting before anyone can mortify us further.

My mind wanders to another time, another moment, as the meeting drones on. We were thirteen, and my family just arrived for the summer. I eagerly stomped up the steps next door, where Emma's mom told me Emma and her sister Audrey had taken a walk to the pop-up shops. I took off on my bike. As my tires rumbled along the boardwalk planks, I sighted the Blackwell girls. They were taller than last time. Audrey looked mostly the same, but Emma had transformed. I slowed. Why hadn't I thought of this? Many girls in my grade had gone through growth spurts, leaving most of us boys behind to look like children among women. Mom said that's how it sometimes worked. Girls often had a growth spurt at an earlier age than boys.

Emma was tall and... beautiful.

And I felt small as I plucked up the courage to get off my bike and walk it to join them. Would things be like they always were?

"Hey, guys." I gripped my handlebars.

Both girls turned to me, smiles lighting their faces. Emma had braces.

"Bryson!" they yelled, stumbling into me for hugs. Yep, things could be the same.

They stepped back, and I smiled, closing my lips over my crooked teeth.

"Hey, look," Audrey said. "Emma's taller than you now."

Emma's cheeks pinked. "Yeah, I'm taller than most of the boys in my grade."

Be cool. "Don't worry. I plan to catch up soon. How's the weather up there, by the way?"

She squared her shoulders, peering down her nose at me. "Pretty good. I'll let you know if it starts raining."

We laughed, and they gave up shopping to walk with me to the hill that slopes down to the beach.

Emma grinned, glancing my way, and my heart did a strange backflip. "Sandcastle contest later? Loser buys gelato."

"You're on. Get your money ready."

There was that backflip again. A feeling that this summer may be more interesting than any before it flooded me like a hard summer rain.

Emma shifts next to me, bringing me back to the present as her shoulder bumps into mine.

"Sorry," she mouths.

I straighten in my seat—several inches taller than her, I might add. Two years later, when we were fifteen, I passed her for good. It was her turn to be surprised when we met up that summer.

Those summers were golden bright spots in my eternal adolescence. But Bill was wrong. We never dated. Never even held hands. Not even once.

There were times when something might have sizzled under the surface, but I was too scared to act on it. Now, I doubt she ever saw me that way.

And now she hates me. I cross my arms. Maybe I hate her too—for hating me for something that happened three years ago.

"The event's less than two weeks away." Mr. Johnston slaps his hands together. "We'll host an outdoor movie on Friday, pop-up shopping, and a cornhole tournament on Saturday as well as a hayride, crafts, and carnival games. Of course, we'll have food trucks, and the event ends with a live band and dance on Saturday night. The building committee is new this year. We've hired a couple of guys to build a bandstand, which will also be utilized throughout the year for future events."

Next, he sends the heads of the committees, including Cole, to separate corners of the room and encourages everyone to find a place to help. Emma rises and heads toward the carpenters.

"Bryson, why don't you help with face painting?"

I swing my gaze to Cole when I hear my name. "Um, I am not artistic. You don't want me doing that."

"Okay. How about you, Olivia?"

"Sure, sounds good."

Cole taps his pencil on his clipboard, paces, and gives out more jobs to others in our group.

My gaze slips to Emma. She's way out of her league over there.

Apparently, Mr. Johnston agrees because he's leading her to our corner. "We're looking for people with their own drill for that committee."

Mrs. Davis, who happens to be hovering nearby, says, "She's an excellent photographer. And she has her own camera."

"Perfect!" He turns back to Emma, whose lips are pressed into a hard line. "I'd love for you to be the official photographer. You can document the event, and we'll share the photos on social media."

"Uh... sure. Okay."

"And maybe set up a self-serve photo booth. That would be nice."

Cole, still intent on his mission, stops in front of me. "Bryson, you can be in charge of collecting the supplies we need for crafts, and then on the festival day, you can operate the kids' fishing game. Oh, and you'll need to make the backdrop ahead of time. And paint it to look like the lake."

"Again, Cole, I'm not artistic."

"Emma can help you with that," Mrs. Davis pipes up again. "She's very artistic, aren't you, sweetie?"

Emma's mouth drops open under wide green eyes. She closes it. Opens. "Um, I don't—"

"Great, it's settled," Mr. Johnston slaps his hands again. "You can help with whatever this boy needs, along with your photography duties."

Cole glances between Emma and me and chuckles as he marks our names on his clipboard. "Yep. That's perfect."

12

Emma

"Wait. What?" I sputter. "But—"

Mema touches my shoulder as her electric blue earrings quiver against her neck. "Oh, this will be the best fall festival ever. You'll be perfect for these artistic jobs. Let me know if you need anything."

Seriously? I can't believe this. I've been duped. By Mema.

As she saunters away, she winks in my direction.

She intends to force Bryson and me to play nice. Or... is she trying to set us up?

I groan.

McDoom shifts and raises a brow as if to say, "Am I that bad?"

An image of myself clinging to cold metal high above the ground pops into my mind. Red and blue lights flashing below.

I ball my hand into a fist. *Yes. Yes, you are.*

Maybe I can make a run for it, but I'm already behaving like a child. Better not to make things worse.

Plus, Mema's blocking the door.

Cole taps his clipboard again. "It's loud in here. Should we go somewhere else?"

Olivia stands and grabs her shoulder bag. "Let's go back to Coffee Connection. We can get drinks and a table and make our plans."

Cole agrees and starts for the door with our other committee volunteers.

Olivia's smile falters at my hard look. When Bryson crosses his arms, she glances between us. "Okay, you two. I don't know what happened way back when, but you need to give it a rest. From my understanding, whatever it was happened years ago. Time to move on."

Bryson gestures toward me. "I've moved on. She hasn't."

Of all the! I nearly stamp my foot—yeah, childish, remember? "You're not the one who was betrayed."

His arms slip to his sides. "Betrayed? Are you serious? I—"

"Okay, whatever." Olivia slides a finger across her neck. "Friendship dead. The bottom line, though, we all have to work together. Can you at least be—cordial or something? Please? For the rest of us?"

"Fine."

"Fine."

Olivia shakes her head and leads us out the door and onto the sidewalk. I put as much space between Bryson and me as possible without actually walking in the gutter. We pass the pavilion where the building committee has relocated, and there he is—McDarcy—all muscles and smolder, deep in discussion over blueprints.

Bryson frowns when he catches me staring, but he says nothing. I should have never let Bryson see me talk to the carpenter. When he showed up, I should've turned right around and saved it for another day.

My back to McDarcy, I continue up the street.

Fail. Again.

At the café, Cole veers toward the coziest corner spot. "I'll snag the couches while you order."

Minutes later, I'm nestled between Olivia and Bryson, cradling a steaming mug of pumpkin spice latte. I angle toward Olivia and inhale the familiar scent, hoping it will melt the knot lodged in my stomach.

"Okay, so for crafts." Olivia flips through a notebook filled with way-too-ambitious ideas. "Maybe we could paint mini pumpkins. Might be less messy than carving?"

I nod but stay silent as the others discuss options. I'm hyperaware of the boy sitting next to me. Bryson leans back against the plush cushions, one arm draped over the armrest.

Don't think about the past.

I can't help it.

It was the first day of our last summer in Carlton Landing. I was fifteen years old and sitting on this very couch. I planned to finish reading the novel I started on the car ride over and, most importantly, wait for Bryson to arrive.

We'd communicated more in the last year than we ever had during the school year, texting, sending photos and memes, and even talking on the phone a few times. We'd been messaging all day, and his family was only hours away.

That's why I sat up abruptly when he walked by the café sidewalk only fifteen minutes later. He was heading toward Mama Tig's, which was where I told Mom I was going before I discovered how crowded it was.

He's trying to sneak up on me.

I bit my lip to keep it from turning up into a sappy smile. He was at least two inches taller than last time I saw him. He was wearing a snug gray Eagles Cross Country T-shirt, and he'd let his clean-cut hair grow out into a shaggy I-care-but-I-don't-care style.

He looked… good.

I smoothed out my dark hair and thumbed out a text.

Me: How much longer? I'm bored.

He pulled his phone from his swim trunks pocket and smiled—no more braces.

Bryson: Maybe an hour

Cute little liar.

Bryson: What are you up to?

Hmm. What should I say?

Me: I got a drink, and now I'm heading to the dock.

I grabbed my sweet tea and stood. There. Not a lie.
He stopped and turned the other way toward the dock.
I giggled, and someone working on a laptop nearby looked up.
"Sorry," I mouthed.

Bryson: Cool. I'll text when we get there.

Uh-huh. I sent a thumbs-up.
When he passed, I followed him all the way to the lake, ditching my things under a tree. He crept along the footbridge leading to the dock, trying to peek between the boats, searching for me. When a Jet Ski cranked its engine, I slipped behind him and covered his eyes.

"You thought you could sneak up on me?" I laughed as I pushed him toward the edge of the bridge. But he was stronger than I remembered, and he twisted around, chuckling, and grabbed my wrist, tugging me with him. "If I'm going in, you're going—"

And then we're both underwater.

We could both reach—as I knew we could—and when we broke the surface, we splashed each other like a couple of elementary kids.

"I. Can't. Believe. You. Did. That." He said each word with a spray of water. "I could have dropped my phone!" Luckily, he was laughing and still clutching it.

I made a face. I didn't think of that. "Oops."

We heaved ourselves out and lay on the dock to dry off. We chatted like the old friends we were, picking up right where we left off.

Only… this time, I was distracted in ways I'd never been with him before. Like the way the water dripped from his hair to roll down his angled cheek. Or how his hand felt when he gripped mine to help me to my feet. Or how my heart thundered when he glanced my way on our stroll home.

Later, our families caught up over dinner. Mema asked Bryson if he had a girlfriend. He spluttered about a girl he was "just talking to," so I shoved those distractions to the back of my mind. I locked them up and threw away the key.

I had to let it go.

I needed to.

"Emma, what do you think?" Cole's voice pulls me back.

I straighten. "Um… Sure. Yeah. Everything sounds good."

He goes on to say something else as my phone buzzes in my pocket.

Mom: Been trying to call you. The Thomas family has decided to head to Carlton Landing in TWO days. You need to clean up and move in with Mema ASAP. Write back to confirm you saw this.

Just super.

Cole rips a paper from his notepad and dangles it before my face. "Here's the list of supplies. You two should get started on the backdrop for the fishing game as soon as possible."

I snatch it from his fingers. "Can't wait."

"Neither can I," Bryson says. "Super fun."

13

Bryson

"Seriously? She bailed? Again." I clatter my phone onto the kitchen counter, earning a side-eye from Mom. Emma's text was even secondhand. She blocked my number back in the day, so she had to tell Olivia to tell Cole to tell me she couldn't go shopping for supplies today. And now she's bailing again. Not that I was super excited about any of it. It's the principle of the thing.

"She's so annoying."

"She certainly gets under your skin." Mom winks and hands over a plate of scrambled eggs and pancakes. "It's breakfast for dinner tonight."

I take it and follow her onto the front porch. We sit on either side of a round table. The sun is sinking low on the horizon, and the patch of lake visible between the trees sparkles in the distance. There's a chill in the air, so she turns on the heat lamp.

Tyler is already seated before a plate of pancakes made into an elaborate face with chocolate chips and whipped cream.

"Hey," I say. "You never made me pancakes like that. And definitely not for dinner."

She smooths Tyler's hair back out of his eyes. "Grandkids are meant to be spoiled."

Tyler scoops a forkful of whipped cream into his mouth. "Where's Papa?"

Mom unfolds a napkin and wipes his mouth. "Remember, he's going on a business trip for a while. He left with Cole's dad super early before you woke up."

"Oh, yeah."

We eat in silence until Mom shivers and then stands to adjust the heat lamp. "I'm sure there's a good reason Emma canceled. Give her the benefit of the doubt."

I stab my eggs. "Doubt it. She just doesn't want to be around me."

"Oh, surely not."

"I'm almost positive that's it."

She makes a dismissive noise as she returns to her seat.

My current feelings toward Emma didn't stop me from staying up late the last two nights reading the YA rom-com she published. I bought it and downloaded it to my phone the first chance I got. A romance novel is not my first choice of reading material, but knowing she wrote it keeps me coming back.

Movement catches my eye through the wooden railing around the porch. Hmm. It's the author herself. Emmie Blackwell carries a box up the sloping street toward us.

Mrs. Davis steps out on their porch wearing a leopard-print sweatshirt to wave at her. Catching sight of us, she says, "Good evening, Dumars! How are you today?"

Mom swallows and wipes her mouth with a napkin. "Hey, Wanda. We're fine." She nods toward Emma. "What are you guys up to today?"

"Oh, Emma's moving in. There's a renter for the house she's staying in, and they'll arrive in the morning. She's been working to get it ready all day."

"How nice to have her next door again."

"Yes, I'm looking forward to it." Mrs. Davis turns away.

Mom mouths, "See? Benefit of the doubt."

I frown and cut a bite of pancake with my fork.

As I chew, Emma struggles under her load.

Mom's gaze bores into me. "You know, Bryson, helping her might be a good first step toward mending whatever fence broke between you two."

"Mom, the fence burned down. It's irreparable."

She lets her suggestion hang. I shift in my seat as it refuses to be swatted away like an annoying mosquito.

She picks up her coffee mug. "Maybe it needs to be rebuilt. And kindness doesn't need an invitation."

I roll my eyes skyward. Ugh. I hate it when she's right.

A clatter echoes down the street where the bottom has fallen out of the box Emma's carrying. Books and trinkets scatter over the sidewalk.

I push from the table and trudge inside for the golf cart keys.

Tyler hops off his chair and trails after me. "I'll help."

"Grab a few grocery bags from the pantry," Mom calls. "And don't roll your eyes at me."

"Yeah, Uncle Bryce," Tyler adds.

The Oklahoma breeze toys with my hair as we cruise up the street.

Emma's shoulders droop when we pull up next to her. "Of course, it's you here to catch me at a low point."

I should turn right around. But then, kindness doesn't need an invitation.

"This isn't a low point. This is a collapsed box."

"You don't have to help me."

"It's okay. Besides, Mom's making me."

"No, she's not." Tyler glances back at Mom, who waves from her seat on the porch. He and I need to discuss keeping things to ourselves.

Emma almost smiles. "What's your name?"

"I'm Tyler."

"Tyler? As in Tyler, who was a baby last time I saw you?"

"I'm not a baby. I'm five."

"Oh, you're all grown up."

I step from the golf cart. "Yeah, this is my sister's son. He's staying with us for a few weeks."

"Wow, nice to meet you, Tyler."

She sticks out a hand, and Tyler shakes it, beaming.

"You too." He blinks up at me, as super serious as only a five-year-old can be. "Is this the complicated girl?"

Her eyebrows shoot high on her forehead.

Oh, boy. We really need to have that talk.

But what better way to describe us? I shrug. "Yep. Most definitely. Come on, buddy. Let's pick this stuff up."

I jump down and hand each of them a reusable grocery bag. Tyler and I stack books as Emma gathers scattered photos of her with people I don't know.

"Complicated, huh?"

I freeze. She's looking at me with something other than loathing, and her green-eyed gaze traps me. I don't break her stare. "Tell me I'm wrong."

She lifts a shoulder but doesn't disagree.

We scuttle around, gathering her things, each step a tentative dance move, one wrong beat away from a full-on stumble into awkwardness. After depositing her things on their front porch, we make a trip to her old house and back gathering more bags, boxes, and a ridiculous pot holding fake yellow flowers. Once everything is delivered, she arranges the flowerpot on the porch and tries to shoo us away, but Tyler insists we carry the rest up the stairs.

The tension doesn't dissolve, but it transforms into something softer, following us up at a distance in a way that could be forgotten for a moment or two.

The past whispers between the creaks of the wooden steps, and the corner of my mouth turns up. I shift the weight of the box I carry. "Remember when we almost managed to sled down this staircase?"

Emma doesn't turn, but I hear a quiet laugh.

Tyler stomps behind me, holding two books. "Can I try it?"

"No." Emma and I say at the same time.

I laugh, and when Emma reaches the landing, she turns back. "What were we thinking? We never would've made it without destroying something—or ourselves. Good thing Mom stopped us."

I pause midstep. It's the first time she's smiled at me in three years. She moves around the corner, and my heart hammers in my chest—something familiar and unwanted pulses there.

Stop. She hates you. Don't do this to yourself. Again.

I shake the memory away and drop my box in a light, airy room that will now be Emma's. "So... our moms talked on the phone."

She pauses. "Uh, yeah. Apparently, my mom felt the need to catch up after she learned your family's here."

"Ah." Since then, Mom's been all too happy to bring Emma up every five seconds. What did they talk about? Emma won't tell me, so I carry two more boxes up as she unpacks.

"Hey, is that you at graduation?" I reach for a photo on the smooth white desk, but she snatches it away before I can grab it. Her open expression closes off.

Yikes. "What? Did I say something?"

"No, it's just—graduation is a sore subject."

Tyler darts toward the double doors across the landing. "Can I look at your balcony?"

Emma tucks the photo under a book. "Sure."

We follow him out where gold from the low evening sun bathes the open space.

Nostalgia hits me like an August Oklahoma heat. There are so many memories: being banished here when we came in wet from the lake, messy crafts, popcorn, movie nights, board games around the coffee table... lounging in the shade. My gaze drifts to the love seat.

And then there's that memory.

The one that's haunted me.

It was that summer. The last one. Just before he arrived.

I'd been talking to this girl back home. We weren't together or anything, but we texted some. But when I arrived in Carlton Landing, I knew there was no hope for her. I barely thought about her at all. Not with Emma around.

One summer evening as the sun drifted to the horizon, Emma and I crowded around the coffee table with Audrey, their cousin Will, and several others for a card game. Emma sat sandwiched between me and another kid, and after we finished up, everyone ran off to play hide-and-seek, leaving us alone in the warm Oklahoma breeze. The air seemed to charge with electricity. Would she move away?

She didn't.

A gust of wind, carrying the scent of fresh-cut grass and a distant barbecue, blew her hair across her face. I reached up to push it away at the same time she did. Our eyes locked. Did she lean in? Or was it me who inched closer?

I'd just glanced down at her lips when my phone vibrated between us. She scooted away, and I picked it up.

Nora: Hey, handsome. Miss me?

Emma's face closed off, and she stood. "I'm going to find Audrey." She spoke in her usual tone as if nothing had sparked between us.

I stood as she reached the door. "Emma—"

"I'm hungry." She cut through my words. "Maybe we can talk our parents into taking us to Mama Tig's later."

"Yeah, sure, but—"

And she was gone. She practically sprinted down the stairs.

One week later, *he* showed up.

Eric Tucker.

The boy who started a chain reaction that ended in a broken friendship. I ball my hand into a fist.

Tyler hums an off-key tune, bringing me back to the present, and I shake out my hand.

Emma's staring at the love seat too.

Our gazes lock, and there it is—the tension, the unspoken questions. Did you feel it too? Why didn't we ever talk about it? Her eyes search mine, and my heart thumps a rapid rhythm. I struggle to maintain my cool facade.

What was my goal again? Oh yes. Entertain myself by annoying her. Get back to it.

But before I can think of anything to lighten the mood, she turns away. "Tyler, your hair is glowing. The sun is hitting it just right."

He reaches up to touch his head. "It is?"

"Yeah, you know why?"

"Why?"

"This is what we call the golden hour. It's the time of day with the very best sunlight. At least for photos, anyway. When the low sun casts a golden glow over everything."

"Can you take my photo?"

"Sure. Hang on." She steps back inside and returns with her camera. "Smile."

He displays a toothy grin. "Cheese."

She snaps a few shots and then kneels at his level. "Take a look."

I peek over his shoulder. The photos are perfect.

"Cool," Tyler says.

Emma stands, snapping the lens cap back on. "Well, I better get my room cleaned up." She ruffles Tyler's hair. "Thanks for helping." She turns my way, and the sun bathes her skin in golden light, brightening her green eyes to a brilliant shade. Her voice lowers. "Both of you."

I stuff my hands in my pockets. "You're welcome."

"No problem." Tyler raises his hand for a high five, so I oblige.

We step inside, and she grabs her notebook to thumb the pages as I've seen her do before. "I can't help with the festival stuff until later in the day tomorrow. I have to be at Coffee Connection at six a.m." She makes a face.

"Okay. I'll see you tomorrow afternoon, then. Prepare to be wowed by my *artistic ability*."

"Oh, I remember your so-called artistic ability."

I chuckle and mentally stomp on my heart when it tries to skip around because she did something so small as remember something about me.

Tyler and I head down the stairs, and, bless him, the kid says in a not-so-quiet voice. "She's not so complicated."

I shake my head and move him along out the front door.

Not true, kid. Not even close.

14

Emma

"Here you go, Mrs. Jenkins." I pass over a photo-worthy café mocha topped with whipped cream and chocolate drizzle. "Enjoy."

Now that we've caught up on the early morning crowd, Joanna heads to her office in the back, and I refill the sugar packets.

My phone chirps with a message.

Audrey: Hey, sis. Don't forget I'll be there on Friday. Morgan and Will decided to join me. Do you need me to bring anything?

Muscles I didn't know were tense relax. Smiling, I text back.

Me: I can't wait! And it will be great to see the lovebirds. Could you bring my orange and red scarf from the hallway closet?

Audrey: No problem. I'm so excited! *heart* See you then!

I send a video of a dog watching for visitors out his front window.

The early morning is slow after the initial rush. An hour later, when I've done all my chores and there are no customers, I pull out my laptop and ring up a pumpkin spice latte for myself—using my employee discount, of course. The heart shape on top is so perfect I arrange it next to my keyboard, snap a photo, and then post it to Instagram with the caption, "Pumpkin spice makes writing so nice." While there, I scroll through photos, most of which are of my high school friends having fun at college. That should be me. Eventually, I swipe a Carlton Landing post onto my screen.

There's a recycled photo of their last neighborhood dinner with the caption, "Residents and visitors, it looks like this weekend will bring fabulous weather. We want to take advantage, so plan to join us for a family dinner under the main pavilion on Friday night. Smitty's Smokehouse is catering. Bring your family, bring a date, bring your friends. Space is limited. Purchase your spot today. (Link in bio.)"

Sounds fun. I've never been to one of those dinners.

I text Audrey to see if they want to come, and five minutes later, she lets me know the three of them are in.

Audrey: Oh, and you should invite that Darcy guy.

What?

Me: It's McDarcy. And… I don't know him that well.

Audrey: That's the point. It could be a date, only you don't have to carry the conversation, because we'll be there.

Me: I don't know.

Audrey: Well, think about it. It might make great novel material.

I toss my phone in my purse.

Ask McDarcy to the dinner?

Now I'm nauseous. But she's right. It *would* be great material. The girl asks the guy. An unusually warm fall evening. Good food and a long walk afterward. This has potential both in real life and in my novel. Maybe this is where I run my fingers through his tousled hair.

Then, without my permission, Bryson's tousled hair appears in my mind… along with his questioning face.

He's there, standing on that balcony with an expression that wonders if I remember. Do I recall the golden sunlight? The slight breeze? Leaning in?

Of course I remember. My feelings on that balcony were confusing—in the past and yesterday.

But there was that text message from the other girl. And then other things that happened weeks later still make my blood boil.

Ugh. I can't let Bryson soften my mood toward him.

Best to put him out of my mind and get back to work.

Around nine o'clock, McDarcy's truck arrives, and he saunters inside the house next door.

Do I have enough guts to go over there once my shift ends? Asking him to build a Little Free Library is one thing. Asking him on a date is something totally different. Am I brave enough?

We'll see.

Two hours later, Olivia sprints in for her shift. We overlap during the lunch hour, but business is slow on a Wednesday, so we have plenty of time to hang out.

She catches me staring out the window—again—and pauses next to me, arms crossed. McDarcy is using a power drill, but really, it wasn't him I was thinking about.

"So what's the plan?" she asks. "Have you tried giving him the blueprints again?"

"No, not yet. But I will. I guess. Maybe."

"There's the confidence I love."

I bump her shoulder. "My sister wants me to ask him to the family dinner on Friday."

"Whoa. Are you?"

"Maybe."

"Are you the sunshine character or what? Do it."

As my shift ends, Bryson's mom arrives with Tyler. "Hey, Emma," she says. "We were getting stir-crazy at home. Thought we might get a fun drink and play Chutes and Ladders for a while."

Tyler's holding the box and shakes it when I look his way. "Will you play with us? It's more fun with extra people."

"Oh, I don't—"

"Please," he whines, arranging his features into a sad puppy face. How am I supposed to say no to that?

"Okay. Sure. One game." I hold up a finger, and a heart-melting smile crosses his face. He looks like his mom. And his uncle Bryson.

They order, and we set up the game.

On my third turn, I flick the arrow and then have to slide back almost to the beginning.

I frown at my game piece as the door dings.

"Uncle Bryce!" Tyler jumps up and hugs him like he hasn't seen him in a month. "Where've you been?"

"Hey, buddy." Bryson narrows his eyes at our cozy corner. "I was checking with a builder up on Ridge Line to see if they had some extra wood we could use. No luck yet."

Tyler returns to his chair. "Can I help you paint it when you get it?"

"Probably not, but I'll get you your own to paint."

"Yay. Come play with us. Emma's losing, so she won't mind starting over."

I scoot my chair back. "Bryson can take my place."

"No, please." Tyler presses a hand on my shoulder. There's that puppy face again. "Four is the perfect number."

I relent because, well, I'm weak.

We play, and I find out I'm the most unlucky Chutes and Ladders player in all the world.

There's not really any skill involved. Only spinning and landing on the number of spaces I should move. Tyler has the best luck of all and wins. He insists the rest of us play it out. Mrs. Dumar takes second.

Tyler bounces in his seat. "Keep going."

Mrs. Dumar wanders down the hall to my bookshelf, and after another minute, Bryson and I have both slid back down the board. Will this game ever be over?

Tyler leans on the table. "Uncle Bryce is reading a book you wrote."

My gaze shoots to Bryson. "No. You said you wouldn't."

"I certainly did not."

"But I asked you not to."

"And I told you I was buying it."

I press my lips together. There's nothing I can do short of stealing his phone. And I'm above that. Right?

Tyler cocks his head. "Why don't you want him to read it?"

Bryson raises a brow, and a muscle ticks in my jaw. I don't have a valid reason. "I just don't."

An irritating smile crosses Bryson's lips at my childish reply. He shrugs and spins the wheel again.

There's no reason for me not to want anyone to read *that* novel. But… it's Bryson. McDoom. It's a violation for my enemy to read my words.

We say nothing more about the book, and Tyler's attention wanes. He joins Mrs. Dumar to browse the bookshelf where I've stocked a few children's books.

Bryson groans as his game piece lands on another chute. "This might never end."

"Why are we so bad at this?"

"Speak for yourself."

"Look at the board!"

When mine lands on yet another shoot that will take me almost to the beginning of the game, Bryson grabs my hand, electricity shooting between us. "Nope." He forces my character near the top and pitches his voice toward the hallway. "Four, five, six. Oh look, Tyler. Emma won."

He comes running over. "Yay. I knew you could beat him."

I hold my hand for a high five. "Yep, me too. He's terrible."

Tyler slaps my palm as Bryson says, "I'm terrible?"

"Yeah, I mean, look. The proof is before your eyes."

Bryson shakes his head and stands, but movement out the window catches my attention. McDarcy is hauling lumber out his door.

Bryson follows my gaze and then smirks as if to say, *"Really? Him?"*

Yes, really.

I pluck the blueprints from my backpack. "I'll ask if he has anything we can use for the fishing game."

"That's my job."

"That's okay. I want to."

He doesn't smile at this.

I hustle out the door with three objectives: plywood, library, Friday night dinner… and irritating Bryson. Okay, that was four.

Once again, I've put myself on display. No doubt they're all watching me. I will not cower.

But when I turn the corner, Cole is already talking to him.

"Sure." McDarcy is saying. "I can show you what I have. Come on."

They trudge up the steps, and Cole turns back before entering. "Oh hey, Emma. They have some extra plywood. I'll get some for the fishing game."

And then they're gone, leaving me to stand by myself. By the porta potty.

Super.

When I turn toward the café, Bryson stands on the porch, arms crossed. The breeze rustles his light-brown hair. Tyler is at his side, mimicking his stance.

Bryson's mouth twitches, and I'm not sure if those lips leave me wanting to punch them or do something else entirely.

My own turn down.

Bryson chuckles. Tyler copies him. "Maybe you need a wingman. Someone other than Cole."

Definitely, punch.

15

Emma

Last night, Bryson and I managed to paint a blue base coat on the wood slab without killing each other. He might've even forgiven me for having to work while he bought all the supplies. I call it a win.

Luckily, Cole and Olivia were at the painting session to carry the conversation as they updated an old cornhole set to a lovely pumpkin color.

Mema's backyard became the art studio, and now everything is drying on the screened-in porch.

I got to sleep in today but gave up on trying to work on my manuscript as Mema blasted music while vacuuming. That woman—love her—but she is not quiet.

Once she left, I locked in to work, and by lunchtime, I'd written a few words. Now, however, as often happens these days, I'm stuck. Writer's block has stilled my fingers, and I need inspiration. Badly.

And I've concocted a new plan.

Olivia is on shift at Coffee Connection, so I swing by to run through my idea. "Most of the time, he eats lunch on the dock. This time, I'll already be there eating mine. I'll ask him to join me and look over my blueprints. I even brought an extra brownie I can offer him."

"Good plan. It has potential." She adjusts her off-the-shoulder top and then flicks a crumb from the bar. "But why not take the papers to him right now?"

"Because I'm tired of having an audience whenever I try to talk to the guy. As sure as I walk over there, *someone* will show up."

"Like… a particular someone, or—"

"No. No one in particular. Just anyone."

She grins. "Okay, well, have fun."

I grab the sack lunch I brought. "Meet-cute, take three, here I come."

Olivia pats my head. "How can it be a meet-cute if you've already met? Twice. And sat in a meeting together."

I swat her hand away. "We haven't met. I still don't know his name."

"Oh, it's—"

I clamp my hand over her mouth. "Don't tell me. That's the one shred of truth I'm hanging on to."

"Okay, fine."

I push open the café's front door. Ding. "Wish me luck."

"Good luck. Try not to be too creepy."

I laugh and give her a thumbs-up.

I take my time strolling down to the lake and then cross the footbridge to the boat dock, snapping photos as I go. These will be great for Instagram. I meander down the wooden planks until I reach the end where a sundeck stretches over the water. This is usually where McDarcy sits with his legs dangling off the edge. Good. He's not here yet.

Hopefully, he'll show up. If not, I give up.

Why's it so difficult to hire a hot carpenter to build a Little Free Library? I mean, really?

I sit under the metal roof near a purple wake boat and eat the apple from my sack.

The wind kicks up, and it's not quite warm enough to feel truly pleasant. I zip my jacket, and the gate clangs. Footsteps vibrate toward me. Is it him? I want to look, but it would be ridiculous if he saw me peeking over the purple boat. I swing my feet to hang from the wood planks like he does, pull my turkey sandwich from the bag, and take a bite.

It now sounds like several sets of feet stomping my way.

Great.

Maybe it's a group heading out on the water, and they'll jump in their boat and leave.

Nope, they're coming to the end of the dock.

"Emma?"

No, no, no. What's he doing out here? I look over my shoulder. Bryson Dumar moves out of the shade, and the sun illuminates his handsome but annoying face as he squints down at me.

"Bryson." I take another bite.

Cole joins him, and... McDarcy follows. I stop chewing.

The three of them stand over me, staring, so I get to my feet.

"What are you up to?" Cole asks.

I chew the sandwich bite and force it down my throat. "Eating lunch."

Brilliant.

Bryson's gaze bounces between McDarcy and me before he slides a hand along the purple boat's smooth hull. "Cole's about to take us out on his dad's new ride. You should come."

I don't like the look on his face. He thinks I'll say no.

I raise my chin. If McDarcy is going, then I am too. "Sure. Sounds fun."

Cole starts untying a rope. "Cool. You can finish eating on the boat. Hop in."

I look back at Bryson, and he mouths, "Wingman."

Is he serious? "No," I mouth back.

He grins that infuriating grin I remember so well. Ugh.

I settle up front, far away from him.

I love to cruise around Lake Eufaula and have had the opportunity many times. My parents weren't boat people, or at least not enough to buy one and maintain it. So I've always managed to hitch rides with others.

McDarcy hops in. "Thanks for bringing me out, man. I'm trying to talk my parents into buying one."

Bryson boards as Cole moves behind the steering wheel. "No problem. I've been hoping for a decent day to take it out."

McDarcy indicates a storage compartment above the steering wheel. "Care if I check out the capacity?"

Cole cranks the engine. "Have at it."

McDarcy opens several compartments and then wanders to the front where I sit with my legs stretched out on one of the bench seats. He tilts the seat cushion across from me, revealing a spacious area holding life jackets. I lean forward to look in. He closes the compartment, and I stand. "Want to check over here?"

He meets my gaze and smiles. "Sure." He's as happy as a fisherman in Bass Pro Shop. I've never seen this look on his face. Not that I've been keeping track. Much. It's cute.

We each take a side and lift the seat, discovering more life jackets.

When he closes the compartment, I sit with my legs out, and he does the same on the other side.

Bryson, taking the hint, settles on the bench behind Cole.

As we back out of our slip, McDarcy crosses his arms behind his head.

"So what do you think?" I ask. "Does it meet your requirements?"

"Definitely."

Bryson cranks up the music, and McDarcy turns his face the other way toward the lake. The wind tousles his dark hair, and the sun shines across his tan skin. A deep shadow appears where his dimple sinks into his cheek. He runs a hand through his hair, giving a lovely view of his biceps. There are goose bumps across his arms, but he doesn't seem to mind.

I shiver. My light jacket and McDarcy's cool indifference won't keep me warm when we pick up speed.

Bryson tilts his head toward McDarcy. *Go on*, he seems to say.

I roll my eyes and turn back around. I don't need a wingman.

I wait long enough so it's my idea, not Bryson's, then say, "Have you had a chance to think about the library project?"

"Oh right. I forgot about that."

I fish the blueprints from my camera bag, and he reluctantly takes them. "There's a letter from the homeowner association too."

He flips through them. "I'll say maybe for now. I'll look at them later and maybe get you a quote."

Progress! "Okay. Sounds good." Now about the Friday night dinner. Deep breath.

Cole slaps his hand on the dash in time with the song he's playing. "Hey, Kip."

Kip?

McDarcy turns.

"I have all the research my dad and I did while boat shopping. I'll print it out for you. There were several for sale by owners, and some might still be available."

"That'd be great."

"Oh, and the fall festival committee wants to check in about that stage and discuss a few other building projects coming up. You should join Bryson and me tomorrow for this dinner thing the city is having. It's catered by a barbecue place. Most everyone will be there."

McDarcy—Kip, it seems—perks up. "That sounds awesome. I'll be there. We're open to new work."

Oh really?

"Nice." Cole shoves the accelerator forward, and as we speed across the water, my blueprints rip from Kip's fingers and fly away into the wind.

He makes a face. "Uh… sorry."

Bryson laughs.

I grind my teeth but manage to hold in a growl. I'm the sunshine character. Right? Cole stole my date out from under me. Now this. But I smile. "No worries. I'll print out another copy."

"Okay. Bring it by anytime."

This lifts my mood. I have a great excuse to see him again. Maybe this meet-cute—okay, fine, it's not a meet-cute, but perhaps a meet ugly or a meet disaster—is not such a disaster after all.

Cole yells out as he pushes us even faster. I laugh and wrap my arms around my shoulders.

I look back at Cole who's cranked up the volume on an old country song. He's grinning like an idiot, watching the waves ahead.

Behind him, Bryson lounges in the back. He's staring out across the choppy water, lips upturned. Is he laughing at me? Is my face in his mind? Just as the wind and sun played across Kip's handsome face, they do the same to Bryson. His sandy hair is wild on the same wind that pulls his long-sleeve T-shirt tight across his chest. He squints into the distance. What holds his attention? Our ride sends waves that ripple for ages. A flock of birds flies low over our wake.

I rub my freezing arms.

When I turn away from the disappearing birds, Bryson's watching me. He stands, opens the compartment he was sitting on, and grabs a beach towel. He tosses it my way, but it whips back at his feet. We both laugh, and he brings it to me.

I wrap it around my shoulders. "Thanks."

He nods and returns to his seat, and I only tear my gaze from his back when I hear a low chuckle. Cole's grin looks as if it's holding a secret, like he knows something I don't. I turn around.

McDarcy, who hasn't glanced my way again, is tipping his head back, eyes closed.

Right. Stay focused. Sunshine. I lean back, close my eyes, and enjoy the wind on my face.

We cruise around for a long while.

Perhaps too long.

By the time the dock comes into view, I'm seasick—er, lake-sick?—and freezing. We turned into the wind and cut across the choppy water to head back. Other boats zip around, creating even more waves for us to pound over.

I clutch the towel around me. No way will I throw up in front of these guys.

As we taxi into our spot, I have one goal. Get on a nonmoving surface. Technically, the dock is floating, but it's not moving nearly as much as the boat.

I stand at the same time McDarcy gets to his feet. We're face-to-face.

He laughs. "Whoa. Your hair is crazy."

I frown but don't speak. I will not throw up.

He runs a hand through his. "How's mine?"

It's also wild. But a good kind of wild. Carefree. Beautiful.

The boat lurches after another boat taxis by. My stomach lurches with it. "I need to get off this boat." I turn toward the dock.

McDarcy laughs, and Bryson touches my elbow to steady me. "Hey, you don't look so good."

"Yeah, I heard." I step onto the bench and then the dock, his hand still supporting me.

"You okay?" Bryson drops his hand.

"I'm good." It's better on the dock, but I need dry land.

"You go on up. We'll tie it off."

I nod and walk back down the line of boats and across the footbridge. When I'm out of eyesight, I pick it up to a jog and run to the café. It's closer than my house. I burst through the door—ding—and race across to the bathroom. Blessedly, the only customers were out on the porch.

Olivia opens her mouth to speak, but her eyes widen at seeing me. "Whoa," is all she gets out before I kick the door shut.

When I emerge minutes later, Olivia's leaning against the wall, arms crossed. She's fighting a smile. "So. How'd it go?"

16

Bryson

"Wow. That's... good."

The fish Emma paints makes mine look like a kindergartner's finger painting. Yikes.

She leans close to the blue slab of wood, chewing on the side of her lip. "Thanks."

"Where'd you learn to do that?"

"Oh, Mema showed me a few tricks. She started painting and taking classes after she retired from teaching. When she came to visit, she'd bring all her supplies and fresh canvases. It became something we always did together."

"I kind of think natural talent might have something to do with it."

She glances at my ridiculous fish blob, suppressing a smile. "Maybe."

"Do you think you could do something with this, or should I paint over it with blue?"

"I'll work on it. Why don't you paint the fishhook?" She nods toward the plan she sketched out. I should have known I was out of my league by that alone. It's an excellent drawing.

And now I'm self-conscious about painting a stupid fishhook. I dip a fresh paintbrush in the soft yellow Emma mixed up earlier and then pause.

She catches my hesitation. "Want me to draw a quick guide?"

I nod, and she pencils in the hook and line. "There, now you can trace it."

Like a kindergartner.

Oh well. I arc my paintbrush over the blue, a shade we decided to go with rather than Lake Eufaula's red-dirt-tinted color. The whole thing looks more like the tropics than an Oklahoma fishing lake. Whatever. The kids will love it.

We work in silence, and she seems content. Happy, even. Sometimes, I believe she honestly dislikes me, and others—like now—that she might want to be friends again. She doesn't laugh with me like she does with Olivia. But maybe we could get there. I search for something to talk about.

"What's your favorite fast food?"

She raises a brow at my lame attempt.

"What? Is that too personal?"

With a hint of a smile, she returns to her painting. "Chick-fil-A. You?"

"I like that one too, but Raising Cane's is my favorite."

I add another coat to the fishhook. "Art used to be your favorite subject in school. What is it now? Or what was it last year?"

"I still like art. But I love creative writing. It was my favorite class. What's yours?"

"Math."

"Which math are you taking now?"

"I'm in an online concurrent calculus class."

Her paintbrush stills. "You're in college-level calculus?"

"Yeah?"

"Hmm. Impressive."

I don't know why, but this makes my lips turn up.

She goes back to her fish. "I'm more of a right-brain kind of girl."

"I know. And, clearly, I'm more left."

"Ah, come on." She points her paintbrush at the fish blob. "This says otherwise."

"Okay, Picasso. Be nice."

We fall back into silence until she asks, "What's homeschooling like?"

"You mean besides doing school in my sweatpants? Honestly, it's pretty chill. There's flexibility to travel, and I get to focus on the subjects I care about."

"Sounds nice. And I bet you didn't have to deal with mean girls or locker-room drama."

"True, but I'm also missing out on some things: prom… cafeteria food."

"Trust me, you're not missing much with the food. Prom was fun, though." She picks up another paintbrush, her laughter like sunlight. This moment feels like it used to. This is why we clicked from the start.

I dip my paintbrush in the yellow. "I miss running on the cross-country team the most. There are homeschool teams, but we moved so much I gave it up."

"But you still run on your own."

"Yeah. How'd you know that?"

"I saw you a few days ago."

I will not be affected by the fact that she noticed me. "Oh." Smooth.

She leans close to the board. "I don't trust people who like to run."

I smirk. "That's fine. You don't trust me anyway."

One corner of her lips turns up. "True."

How much of this statement is us joking around versus the truth? I may never know.

The conversation lulls as we focus on our work, and the afternoon sun casts long shadows across their backyard.

As the chilly air blows across our faces, I glance her way. Something has nagged me since that shadow flicked across her face when I mentioned graduation the other day.

"Emma... why is graduation a sore subject?"

She pauses, her brush hovering midair. The only sound is the wind disturbing the leaves. Then she sets the brush beside the palette.

"Well, I walked with my class at graduation in May, and everything seemed fine then." She rubs a thumb over her paint-splattered palm. "I'd been accepted to OU, and I got my dorm assignment right before I went off to be a counselor at summer camp. Unfortunately, there was no cell service, and we weren't allowed to use phones anyway. When OU got my final transcript from my high school, there was an error. I was one credit short. A tech credit. I could have taken a class this summer, but by the time I heard all the messages they'd left me, summer was almost over, and OU had already dropped me from their enrollment and given the dorm room to someone on the wait-list." She lets out a long breath.

"Oh, wow." I wince. "I'm sorry. I wondered why you weren't off at college. You always talked about going."

"Yeah, I know. I still will. It's not fun watching your friends move on without you." She straightens. "I'm taking an online programming class. So, I'm getting back on track. I'll be done in December." She frowns and grabs her paintbrush. "Hopefully."

"You don't like it?"

"Not really. The professor moves so fast. But it was one of the only classes I could get into in the fall that meets my requirements on such late notice."

"Well, I've taken a programming class. I could help you if you need it."

She swings her wide, green-eyed gaze on me. "Oh no. That's okay. I can handle it."

"Hey, you two." Mrs. Davis pushes through the back door with a tray. "Thought you might like refreshments."

"Thanks, Mema. You didn't need to do that." Emma dips her paintbrush into the water. "But I won't say no."

"Why don't you wash up and join me on the front porch?"

We do as she says and return to find her in the rocking chair, leaving the two of us to share the porch swing.

I accept the iced tea, which is sweet with a hint of apples and spice. "That's good. Thank you."

"You're welcome, honey. I call it autumn iced tea. Oh, here. Have a pumpkin cookie." She nudges the tray toward me across the coffee table. Oh, good. Pumpkin. I glance at Emma, hoping she'll say something like, "Oh, Bryson doesn't like pumpkin flavor." It would be unfortunate, but Mrs. Davis wouldn't allow me to eat one after that.

Emma presses her lips together and raises a brow. Guess not.

I take one, and Mrs. Davis's expectant smile coerces my hand to bring it to my mouth. I brave a bite.

Ugh. It's so bad, but I force a smile. "It's great. Thank you."

Emma makes a choked sound.

Mrs. Davis pats her on the back. "You okay, honey?"

"I'm good. The cookies are excellent. You should send some home with Bryson."

Is she serious?

I stuff the rest of the cookie in my mouth and swallow.

Emma looks impressed.

But then Mrs. Davis places another in my hand. "Here you go, sweetie. Eat up."

"Um, thanks."

Emma's fingers over her mouth cover her mirth.

I bring it to my mouth again.

Emma points behind Mrs. Davis. "There's your mom, Bryson."

As Mrs. Davis and I turn, Emma snatches the cookie and shoves it in her mouth.

Mrs. Davis waves at Mom. I stare at Emma. She shrugs. Did she just do something nice for me?

Mrs. Davis turns back, pleased I've polished off another cookie. "Audrey, Will, and Morgan will be here any minute."

Emma snags another cookie. "Yay! I haven't seen my sister in two months!"

Mrs. Davis tips back in her rocking chair. "It will be nice to have some of the gang back together again. That includes you, Bryson."

I wipe my hands on a napkin. "I look forward to it. I know Audrey and Will, but who's Morgan?"

Mrs. Davis nibbles a cookie. "Morgan is Will's girlfriend. I bet she'll fit right in. Will and Morgan started dating in Carlton Landing. That might be why they like coming back so often. And my other grandson got married here last summer." She sighs dreamily, gazing out across the lawn toward the lake. "Such a great place for romance."

Emma shifts beside me. I don't dare look her way.

Is Mrs. Davis playing matchmaker? Like everyone else.

"You guys finish up. I have more guest prep to do." She stands and saunters inside with her glass of autumn tea, leaving Emma and me sitting close on the porch swing.

Emma rubs her temple and mutters, "Meddling woman."

I'm not sure I was supposed to hear that, but to break the tension, I say, "Maybe the Kip-and-Emma-little-library sparks are about to fly." I cut my gaze to her. "You know, Carlton Landing romance magic and all that."

Her jaw drops.

I'm not sure what made me say it, but her shock might be worth it.

"Kip?" she says.

I can't squelch the coming smile. "Oh, excuse me. McDarcy. I'm taking my wingman job very seriously."

Her eyebrows narrow. "I don't need a wingman! I'm not trying to date him. I'm trying to hire him to build the library."

"Uh-huh."

"I'm... not."

Liar.

She scrunches up her nose. I'm close enough to count each lash and identify every variation of green flecked through her wide eyes. Make that cute liar.

I have got to stop those kinds of thoughts.

We're talking about her and another guy here. Doesn't matter that my heart is doing a happy dance that she's denying she's into him. My mind knows better, but my heart is doing its own thing.

"Emma!"

Our gazes tear away from each other to find Audrey waving furiously from the open window of an old, baby blue Mini Cooper.

Emma shrieks and skips to the top of the porch steps to wait on her sister, who parks, helps her two companions retrieve their bags from the tiny trunk, and rushes up the stairs for a hug. After an overloud reunion, Emma greets the other two, and Audrey saunters my way. She's the same as I remember. The two girls look like sisters. But where Emma has green eyes and is tall enough to come up to my nose, Audrey has brown and stands slightly shorter.

"Bryson Dumar. It's been a while."

"Yes, it has."

We hug, and when I step back, she puts a hand out toward the other two. "You remember our cousin, Will, right?"

"Yeah, of course. Good to see you."

"You too." Will tilts his chin toward the other girl as he threads his fingers through hers. "This is my girlfriend, Morgan."

She waves. "Nice to meet you."

"You too."

Audrey loops an arm through Emma's and starts backing toward the door. Her gaze flits between Emma and me. "Looks like you guys might be mending the old friendship?"

I shrug. "She didn't kick me off the porch."

Emma smirks. "Yet."

"Looks like progress to me."

Emma slings Audrey's bag over her shoulder. "Bryson, let's finish painting later. I want to help them inside."

As they maneuver their luggage over the threshold, Audrey turns back, raising her voice. "A week ago, she told me to call you McDoom."

Emma has the decency to blush while glaring at her sister.

I shove my hands in my pockets. "Did she?"

Audrey nods. "But I don't think I will."

"I appreciate that."

"Will we see you at dinner?"

"Sure. Yeah, I'll be there."

As Emma nudges Audrey through the back door, I hear her say, "You weren't supposed to tell him that."

"What do you care? I thought you hated him."

"I don't—hate him."

I bite my lip to keep from smiling. After all, it's not that great a compliment. But at this moment, it feels like everything.

17

Emma

A smoky barbecue scent mingles with the
conversation and laughter as I lounge at a table covered
in an autumn-themed tablecloth. When our group
arrived, Audrey maneuvered me across from Bryson
and then scampered off with her meal ticket to the food
truck. He pokes a plastic fork at his coleslaw.

Things are weird again now that everyone is here.

He meets my gaze, eyebrows drawn. There's a
question there, but I'm not sure what it is. I'm lost in
those dark eyes until I stand and make my way to
Audrey, sliding next to her in line and pitching my
voice low. "What are you doing forcing me across from
Bryson? I spend enough time with him. Archenemies,
remember?"

As the attendant hands her a plate of chopped brisket, she flips dark hair over her shoulder. "Oops. I thought you guys were on the mend. Sorry."

Like I believe her. I check the J. A. Day while I wait my turn.

Seldom, very seldom, does complete truth belong to any human disclosure; seldom can it happen that something is not a little disguised or a little mistaken. ~ Emma *by Jane Austen*

But, Jane, how are we ever to know the truth if we always hide part of it or misinterpret it?

"Yoo-hoo. Here you go, sweetie."

"Oh. Sorry." I stow my phone and take my plate of barbeque chicken. "Thank you."

Once everyone is seated, Olivia squeezes between Audrey and me for a bottle of barbecue sauce. Strands of light-brown escape the hairdo piled high atop her head and frame her face. Her elbow nudges me, and her breath fogs my ear. "Did you see who's here?" She tilts the bottle toward the fresh-squeezed lemonade stand. Kip is standing there, all gorgeous, waiting in line.

I wipe my sticky fingers with a napkin. "I saw him."

Audrey crowds in, lowering her voice. "That's the carpenter?"

"That's him." Olivia nudges me again. "Tonight's your chance. Pull out your best sunshine character and go get him."

Audrey glances between me and Kip. "Sunshine character?"

Eavesdropping, Bryson rests his elbows on the table. "You know, like the grumpy-sunshine trope in Emmie Blackwell's latest rom-com?"

My gaze whips in his direction. As his smug grin needles me, and I stab a finger in his direction. "Stop reading my book."

He lifts his palms. "Hey, I'm a paying customer."

Audrey laughs. "You're reading Emma's rom-com?"

"You bet. Evan's character speaks to me."

"Evan is a minor side character."

He shrugs.

"Any—way…" Olivia draws out the word. "Don't you guys think Emma should go talk to Kip?"

Audrey frowns in his direction, but Bryson nods. "Definitely. Want me to come with? Wingman reporting for duty."

I roll my eyes. "If I do talk to him, it will be without you. You're not my wingman."

"Suit yourself."

Olivia returns to her seat, and dinner goes on. Kip is deep in conversation with the fall festival event chair, so an opportunity never presents itself.

Bryson seems to be waiting to see what I'll do. Annoying.

Eventually, Audrey cuts through the chatter around us. "Hey, we should play cards on Mema's balcony after dinner. She still has all the old games. Just like old times. This is the first time we've all been here together in ages."

Will rocks back in his chair, dark, shaggy hair flopping over his forehead. "I'm in." He waves his fork at me. "Hey, I just realized this is the first time you've been to Carlton Landing since the"—out come one-handed air quotes—"'incident that must not be named.' Well, not counting Hudson's wedding last summer. I can't believe you live here. I thought you'd never come back."

Oh, great. Thank you, Will, for bringing up the most embarrassing moment of my life. Can I please disappear?

Bryson's mouth opens like he's about to say something, but then closes it—a silent question lingering between us.

When I don't respond, the oblivious Will prods further. "Wasn't that the last time you were here for the summer, Em? What was it, like three years or something?"

"Yep, that's right." I force a smile.

Someone change the subject. Please.

Bryson tilts his head, brow furrowed. "You—never came back?"

No, dummy. I didn't. And it was your fault. Keeping that in, I glare at him.

From further down the table, Olivia stretches toward us. "What was the incident?"

"I'm not sure. Emma got into some trouble, and then these two"—Will points between Bryson and me—"had a gigantic fight, and..." Aha, he *finally* registers the look on my face. His shoulders hunch in. "But maybe we should talk about something else."

I love my cousin, but I'm about ready to dunk him in the lake.

Eyes wide, Olivia taps the table. "No! Guys, what happened? What'd you do?" She's been dying to know since Bryson arrived in Carlton Landing.

I shoot her a murderous glare, and Bryson's gaze returns to me. "Why didn't you ever come back? You love this place."

My heart thunders in my veins. I can't believe this is happening right now. I lower my voice. "I did love this place. But then my best friend betrayed me, and I never wanted to see it again."

Bryson jolts back in his chair like I slapped him, and the strung lights overhead cast a warm glow over his shocked expression. But eventually, his eyes narrow. "You're seriously going to say it's my fault you never came back? And you're still mad at me because I told on you three years ago when you snuck out with some guy we barely knew?"

My fingers have a death grip on my napkin, and Audrey touches my arm. "Hey, let's change the subject."

Will scratches his nose. "I'm sorry. I thought you guys had moved on. You—seemed like you were friends again."

"We're not," I blurt.

Bryson says nothing as the others attempt to steer the conversation out of choppy water. They discuss the boat club, card games, and plans for after dinner, but their gazes don't stray far from me.

What happened? They're wondering.

Not even Bryson knows the aftermath.

I choke my napkin between my fists under the table.

Eventually, the others meander to the dessert table or bend their heads in private conversations.

When no one will overhear, Bryson sits forward. "So that's it? We'll never be friends again?"

"I don't think we can."

He shakes his head. "I can't believe you're still mad at me."

"Of course, I'm still mad at you. It was the worst moment of my life."

He raises an eyebrow as if I'm an overdramatic toddler.

I squeeze my napkin as anger flares up like flames around me. "And you were the one who—"

"Who what, Emma? Who cared about you? Who was worried about your safety? Who wanted your attention?"

I lower my voice. "Wanted my attention? You pushed me away with both hands! I wanted you to hang out with us. You refused." How dare he rewrite history. "And then you tattle-taled. All because you were harboring this unwarranted, toxic friend jealousy."

We've forgotten about the barbecue dinner and the rest of the world as the past crashes into the present.

"I tried to talk to you. To apologize and make it right. But you blocked my number. And it wasn't like we would ever run into each other again. That was it. A five-year friendship gone. You tossed it away like it was nothing because a jealous fifteen-year-old *tattle-taled*."

"Me? You have no idea what you're talking about. You have no idea what happened."

"How could I? You. Blocked. My. Number."

"Because I never wanted to talk to you again. You betrayed me, and I hated you for it."

"Hated me? For telling your parents? I admit, I didn't want you to be anywhere near that jerk. I knew he was trouble. He showed you a different side of himself than he showed me. And he rubbed it in my face that you wanted to be around him more than me."

"No, he didn't. And I didn't want to be around him more than you."

"Emma. Stop. Yes, you did. Your actions proved it. You were both toying with me because you knew I had this enormous crush on you. I was practically in love with you."

The night stills.

I don't move or say a word.

He's frozen, lips parted like he might force the words back into his mouth.

"What?" I can barely whisper.

His shoulders slump, the fight draining out of him. He pinches the bridge of his nose. "Don't pretend you didn't know. Eric did."

I'm shaking my head. My heart races, and my lips part to draw in a much-needed breath.

Cole plops a bowl of banana pudding next to Bryson. I don't hear what they say.

The smell of smoked meat and sweet barbecue sauce fades into the background. This boy I thought I knew, the boy I've been battling as if we're in some endless war, was... practically in love with me?

Cole joins his dad where he and Kip discuss business. I look down at the napkin in my lap.

Love? No. No way. He always kept me at arm's length.

But... the secret smiles, the lingering touches, the arguments that felt more intense than they had any right to be. The almost kiss on Mema's balcony.

The others move on in their conversation. Bryson and I remain quiet. I laugh at the right moments, but I'm not listening. I glance back up at the moment he does. He holds my gaze with those deep-brown eyes. This time, I don't look away. The conversation goes on. Still, our connection doesn't break. My pulse races, and I'm unsure if it's from shock or something else.

Looking at Bryson, really looking, I recognize the same face, the shaggy hair, the straight nose, and the sharp cheekbones, but I see something deeper that I didn't see before.

Or maybe he didn't let me see it.

And what about me? What is it buried deep beneath my layers of stubborn pride?

It's nothing.

Right?

18

Bryson

I do not want to be here. I grip the balcony door and slide it open. Escaping dinner and the stupid words I left hanging between Emma and me was a relief. Then Audrey cornered me and made me promise to come by for cards. Audrey and the others have already gathered around a wicker coffee table.

I take one step through.

Emma's perched on the love seat against the wall. The one with all the memories.

Why did I tell her I was practically in love with her? That should not be the takeaway from a conversation in which the girl you crushed on for years tells you she doesn't want to be friends again—ever.

Now everything is weird. Or more weird than it was before, if possible.

Should I leave before I'm spotted?

Too late. Audrey slides over onto an ottoman next to the coffee table. "Hey, Bryson. I'm glad you came. You can sit here." She indicates the space she's vacated. Next to Emma. On the love seat.

Emma's eyes go wide as I move closer.

Great. She didn't know I was coming. What am I doing here?

I keep my hands stuffed in my jacket pockets, all casual-like. But they're balled up, fighting the urge to do something childish—like pull my phone out and fake a phone call from Mom so I can get out of here.

Cole's suppressing a smile.

Emma scoots to one edge, and I hug the other.

She had no idea how I felt back then. That much is clear. Maybe it never crossed her mind. She never felt the same or looked at me that way.

I'm such an idiot.

"All right, folks! Let's start with Five Crowns." Olivia shuffles and then deals our first three cards. Others gather pen and paper, and I relax as the air fills with laughter and the clinking of ice in glasses of Mema's famous autumn tea.

At least no one is talking about "the incident that must not be named." A minute later, Will's the first one to slap down a set of three stars. He gains no points while I rack up a whopping twenty-eight, putting me in dead last.

It stirs a memory.

It must stir the same in Emma because she says, "Everyone, keep an eye on Will. We caught him cheating a few times back in the day."

Morgan's mouth drops open. "Will! Is that true?"

"Hey, hey, don't believe everything you hear."

I shuffle the cards. "It's true."

Emma laughs for the first time since I walked in the door. "Ha. See."

Morgan mock-gasps. "My boyfriend is a cheater?"

"Okay, fine. I used to cheat. But I'm much more mature now."

"Remember when I caught him with five extra dominoes in his seat?" Audrey says.

We cackle. Just like that, we're kids again. Lost in our own world on the balcony.

But beneath the surface, as memories of past card games dance around us, other memories resurface. Emma and I splitting a Dr Pepper in the afternoon. Sneaking cookies from the pantry. Scratching on Will's window after dark to scare him.

As we finish the last round of Five Crowns, Will tosses his final hand onto the table with a flourish, his grin smug. "And that's how it's done, folks. No cheating necessary."

There's a collective groan. I never made the comeback I hoped for. Well, someone has to be last. Today, that's me.

"Okay, okay, enough with the card games." Olivia adjusts her messy bun. "Let's spice things up with a game of two truths and a lie. It's time we unveil some deep, dark secrets."

Oh, boy.

Morgan bends forward to rest her elbows on her knees. "I'm down for some secret-spilling."

"All right, I'll start." Olivia clasps her hands together. "I once dyed my hair pink, I had my first kiss behind the football stadium at my school, and I can play the ukulele."

Emma laughs. "Well, knowing you, the kissing one is probably true."

Olivia flutters her eyelashes.

"I guess the ukulele," Morgan says, and the rest of us agree to this as a final answer.

Olivia draws a check mark in the air with her finger. "You got it! Emma's right about the kissing, and I dyed my hair pink with Kool-Aid about two years ago. It was awesome, but one time in the pool, it was gone. Okay, who's next?" Her gaze lands on me. "How about you, Bryson?"

I rub my palms on my jeans. "Uh, let's see…" What can I say that has nothing to do with Emma? "I've been scuba diving, I don't like roller coasters, and I've lived in three states in the last four years."

Emma turns in her seat, catching me in the net of her gaze. "The roller coaster one is true. His sister used to bring it up all the time."

I swallow and nod. She remembers that?

"I'm pretty sure he's moved around a lot," Audrey says.

"Okay, let's go with scuba diving as the lie," Will says.

I scooch back. Got 'em. "Nope. I went scuba diving last year. I've moved around a lot, but I've lived in four states in the last four years."

There's a collective groan.

We go around the circle, each offering a mix of fiction and fact, until it's Emma's turn. She yawns. "Pass."

"Oh, come on, Em. You can't back out now."

"I got up super early to go to work this morning. I'm too tired to think of anything."

Audrey flips her ponytail over her shoulder. "Fine. I'll do it for you."

Emma starts to protest, but Audrey shushes her and taps her lips. "Okay. I've got it." She holds up a finger. "Emma always had a secret summer crush back in the day." Another finger goes up. "Her first book was published under a different pen name." A third finger. "And she and Bryson almost kissed on that love seat."

Everyone gasps and laughs.

Emma's face turns scarlet. "Audrey!"

Will cackles, pointing between us. "I knew it!"

The air feels like it's been sucked off the balcony. My heart thumps against my rib cage, a drumbeat of panic.

Emma shakes her head. "That's ridiculous."

Does the fact that I'm the center of kissing attention or that she's denying it annoy me more?

"Is it, though?" Audrey elbows Emma.

"Total fabrication." Emma avoids my gaze.

Will groans, and everyone laughs.

To them, it's a silly story. To me, it was a confusing and devastating summer.

I try to laugh it off. But the memory of that almost kiss—it's all surging back to me, as vivid as if it were yesterday. But was that how Emma saw it? Or was it all in my head? But she must have told Audrey about it. Otherwise, she wouldn't have brought it up.

A voice from below breaks the chatter.

"Olivia, can I come up?"

Olivia hops up, and her grin is as wide as the Oklahoma plains. She lowers her voice, bending toward Emma. "Eek! Don't be mad, but I invited Kip!"

"Kip?" Emma's voice lilts upward.

Her gaze darts my way but then moves back to Olivia as the girl rushes downstairs to meet him. A moment later, he walks in with a confident swagger that screams he knows how good-looking he is. The guy's built like he swings hammers for fun, which, well, he does.

"Hey, guys." His lips curl into a smile that must gain attention wherever he goes.

Audrey looks slightly annoyed. At least that makes two of us.

He saunters over. "Can I sit there?" He points at the only semi-available spot besides the floor—the space between Emma and me.

Emma clears her throat and gives McDufas her perfect smile. "Sure."

He plops down, and I'm fifteen all over again. One minute, I'm sitting next to Emma, having fun, playing cards, and the next, some jerk's sitting between us.

Olivia settles back down. "We were playing two truths and a lie. We've all gone, so it's your turn."

Kip rubs his palms together. "Oh man. I haven't played that since I was twelve. Give me a sec."

Olivia rests her chin on her hand. "Secrets are a good way to go if you don't know what to say."

"All right." He shifts his gaze to the ceiling. "I work with my dad."

Good one, genius. We all already know that.

"I can bench press two hundred and twenty pounds."

I have to strain to keep from rolling my eyes.

"And I played basketball in high school."

"What do we think, gang?" Olivia says.

I say nothing, but the others land on the bench-press one.

"Nope. I didn't play basketball. I played football. I can lift that much."

Cue the eye roll again.

After this, we move on to playing Go Fish like third graders, but it's like I'm watching it through a foggy lens. Kip seems to be getting more comfortable, but Emma laughs too loudly at his jokes. Every time she does, it cranks up the volume on my frustration.

Not that I care. I don't care.

"Emma, you got any threes?" Kip leans close to her.

She smiles and holds her cards where he can't see. "Go fish."

This exchange is getting under my skin more than I'd like to admit. And why should it? It's not like I've got dibs on Emma.… I mean, I've even been offering to be her wingman. But if I'm honest, I never thought he'd give her the time of day. Plus, he's way too old for her.

To be fair, he's treating the other girls the same. But still.

I can't do this. I can't sit here while she flirts with him after refusing any kind of friendship with me, especially after that embarrassing confession of former unrequited love.

And most importantly, I can't let myself fall for her all over again, which is already happening, judging by my reaction. I don't want to end up on the losing side of a love triangle. Again.

So, with a decision that feels like ripping off a Band-Aid, I resolve to steer clear of Emma Blackwell.

I push up from the love seat. "Hey, I'm going to head out."

"Already?" Cole's eyebrows knit together. "We haven't even started Uno."

"Yeah, I'm beat." I force a yawn. "Time to make my exit."

Time to protect my heart.

19

Emma

"Seriously, this weather is bonkers." I bend over to secure my hair in a high ponytail and flip back up to squint into the sky's clear blue expanse. The unseasonably warm day beckons my sister and me onto the water.

Audrey grins back, already sliding her neon orange kayak into Lake Eufaula. "Totally. There's not even any wind. That's Oklahoma for you."

I secure my life jacket with a satisfying snap and drag my green kayak to the red-dirt-stained water's edge. I nudge it out, stepping into the ripples. Yikes. It didn't get the warm-day memo. The water is frigid.

I sit atop the kayak and paddle until I'm gliding and then tip my face to the warm sunlight.

"You okay?" Audrey drifts past me.

"Yeah. I'm fine. It's just… Bryson's avoiding me."

She uses her paddle to angle back in my direction, a smirk in place. She's pulled her dark hair up into a messy bun. "I thought you didn't care."

I dip my paddle into the water again. "I don't. But we have work to do. I mean, we ask him to join us as we work on things for the fall festival, and he only comes when I can't be there. Yesterday, he said he was going on a jog. He could do that anytime. It's rude."

"Weren't you the one avoiding him like a week ago?" I huff.

She smiles, maneuvers her kayak around, and starts paddling. "When I arrived, you two seemed to be getting along okay. Then you argued the other night at dinner. Did something else happen?"

"No." I force my arm muscles to feel the burn with every stroke—time to leave my worries behind on the beach.

"You sure?" Audrey won't let me.

I pause when I reach the middle of this cove and close my eyes. I tip my face to the wind's tickling. When I peek my eyelids open, she raises a brow.

I rest my paddle across my lap. "Fine. Friday at dinner, Bryson said he did what he did back then because he was"—I lift my fingers into air quotes—"'practically in love with me.'"

Her eyes go wide until the corners of her mouth curve up. "I knew it."

"What do you mean you knew it? You didn't know it."

"Of course, he was in love with you. It's so clear now." She giggles, swirling the water with her paddle. "Mom even said once that she thought you two had a crush on each other. She told me to keep an eye on you."

"What? No, she didn't."

"Oh yes, she did. And I seem to remember *you* had an on-again, off-again crush on *him*."

"Maybe. But then he screwed everything up. And forever after it's *off*."

She snorts.

"I'm serious."

"You mean you haven't noticed how cute he is."

"Of course I noticed. I'm not dead."

She giggles again, and our kayaks bump into each other on the calm water.

"I wonder what would happen if you forgave each other."

Anger flares up again. "I didn't do anything. Well, at least not that was any of his business. He got me into a heap of trouble. He has nothing to forgive. He needs to apologize to me."

She presses her lips together but lets my comment go. "Well, maybe you just start with trying to be friends again."

"I don't think we can."

"Why not?"

"Because I literally told him we can't."

"Oh, Emma."

I slap my paddle against the ripples around my kayak. "There are times when I forget what happened. But when I think about it, I get so mad. I'm not sure I can let it go."

Before she can blurt any other mom-like suggestions, I dip my paddle into the water and take off toward the wake zone. "Race you to the buoy."

"No fair. You got a head start." She splashes after me.

Our paddles slice through the water as our laughter spills into the air. I let out a triumphant whoop when I win.

"I don't acknowledge your victory. You cheated, and you have freakishly long arms."

I laugh and stick my tongue out at her. "Jealousy is unbecoming, Audrey."

I exhale, and the tension in my shoulders dissipates. The lake is a calm reddish mirror reflecting the endless Oklahoma sky. A flock of ducks cuts a *V* above the water.

Audrey glides toward the opposite shore where trees with red and gold leaves bend over the water. "Come on. Let's explore over there."

This time, we move slowly as the rhythm of our paddles dips in and out of the glassy surface, creating a hypnotic sound. I pull my cell phone from the dry bag it's sealed in. I was dying to bring out my camera, but that was asking for trouble—and this might be too.

Vivid yellow leaves fall around us, so I carefully capture this postable moment and then turn so Audrey is behind me.

"Selfie! Give me a smile."

She does, and I click away.

I stow my phone—whew—and Audrey diverts the conversation as we continue. "How's the novel inspiration coming along? Your carpenter seemed to have a good time at Mema's."

I'd have preferred her subject change to veer further from romance, but at least we're not talking about Bryson. "Stalled out, if I'm being honest. But yeah, maybe after last night, he at least knows my name. I gave up on arranging the perfect meet-cute. Now, my goal is just to get him to build the library."

"Maybe all the tension between you and Bryson would make good novel material."

I groan. "Our conflicts could fill an entire series, but not of the romance variety."

"Sometimes the best sparks fly from friction."

"Trust me, if our story were a book, readers would throw it across the room in frustration."

She shakes a playful finger. "You sure you're the sunshine character in this story?"

My paddle sends a half-hearted spray of water her way. "Ha ha. Speaking of complicated romances. How are you doing since you found out Drew is dating someone?"

Audrey's paddle hesitates midstroke. "How dare you speak his name."

I laugh. "I'm sorry. But I know it upset you." She only spent the better part of five years pining after him.

"Yeah, it sucks. But I'm okay. I mean, he led me on for years. And then made fun of me for my chronic singleness."

"Jerkface."

"Right? You and I were always a couple of lovesick fools."

"I was not."

"Just because you couldn't—and still can't—admit it doesn't mean it wasn't true. The difference between you and me is I can own it."

"I wasn't!"

She swirls her paddle around a bright-red leaf floating in the water. "Sure. Sure. Anyway. My new lab partner is cute."

"Oooh. Nice. College romance. Maybe I'll use your life for book inspiration. Do you think he'll ask you out?"

"Too soon to tell."

We coast along, and my gaze wanders to the far shore. A familiar figure jogs on the trail. Bryson. His shaggy hair bounces with each stride, and my heart does an involuntary skip before I can reel it back in.

Stop.

"Hey, look, isn't that Bryson?" Audrey asks.

"Yep."

He jogs away, unaware of us.

Audrey's voice breaks the silence, her tone soft. "Do you miss him? His friendship, I mean?"

I run my hands along the paddle resting across my lap. The ripples from our kayaks are the only thing disturbing the water now. I want to say no. But the truth comes pouring out. "Yeah. Sometimes I do. I spent a lot of time being mad at him. But now, being back here... It brings back memories. Good and bad."

"I'm sure it does."

My phone buzzes, and I read the blurry message through the plastic window of the dry bag.

Audrey uses her paddle to swivel around. "What is it?"

"Committee meeting. Cole wants to meet up in a couple of hours." I lean my head back. "That's inconvenient."

"Why? You don't work today, do you?"

"No. But... I was planning to work on my programming homework. Aud, I might fail."

"What?"

"I just don't get it. I have an assignment due tomorrow at midnight, and I don't know how to do it."

She taps her chin with a finger, gaze following the trail where Bryson disappeared into the trees. "Hmm. I wonder who could help you with that."

I brandish my paddle, poised to send a cold splash her way. "Don't you dare say it."

20

Emma

The wind has picked up a notch by the time I drag my kayak through the frigid water and onto the shore. Brrr. Autumn temperatures are set to return this afternoon, and I want to be off the water when they do. We return our kayaks to the rental hut where I retrieve my camera bag and take a few more photos of the fiery hues across the lake.

Audrey unzips her jacket as we trudge up the hill. "Man, I could get used to kayaking every weekend."

I tuck the camera into the bag and slide the strap across my body. "Same. It's an arm workout with a view." I stretch each arm above my head, feeling the pull in my muscles.

"Did you get any good photos with your phone?"

"Yeah. The colors are amazing today." I flip through, pausing on the ones of her.

"Wow. Those are great." She sighs dreamily. "I love fall."

"Thanks."

The device buzzes with my J. A. Day.

What do you have for me today, Miss Austen? I swipe it onto the screen.

Perhaps these offenses would have been overlooked had not your pride been hurt... ~ Pride and Prejudice *by Jane Austen*

Hmm. A little pointed, Jane.

Cole's name flashes on the screen, and I open the text. "You've got to be kidding."

"What?"

I tilt the screen toward her. "Cole says Bryson bailed on the meeting. He's not sure he's going to participate at all."

"Uh-oh."

"He better not use the jogging excuse. I know he's done with that by now."

"Maybe something else is going on."

"I doubt it. I mean. I know he's avoiding me. But this is ridiculous. He's leaving Cole and Olivia hanging. And me! I didn't even want to be on the committee. If anyone gets to quit, it's me."

I thumb a response to Cole, heat bubbling in my chest. But there's also this twist of something else—a sour pinch of responsibility.

Before I can send it, Audrey grips my arm. "Look, I'm happy to help you—to fill in for him if needed—but I don't think you should let Bryson quit, especially if it's because of your past. At least not without talking to him about it. And *before* blasting him over text to his friend. I think he was trying."

I pause. She's right. And I hate it.

"I don't know what to do. Everything is even more complicated now. We hate each other."

"Emma." She faces me, walking backward. "He doesn't hate you. He told you he was in love with you. And I don't think, deep down, you hate him either. You told me so the day I got here."

"Such a fine line between love and hate."

She smirks. "You just told me you miss his friendship. I'm not suggesting you need to date him, but wouldn't it be nice to be in the same room with him without this underlying weirdness? To not have this toxic"—she waves in front of me—"thing weighing you down? You've carried it around long enough."

"It's so annoying when you throw around wise words."

She flips her hair over her shoulder. "Older and wiser. Don't forget it."

"As if you'd let me. Fine. I'll talk to him. But I'm doing this for the sake of the fall festival. And if this blows up in my face, we're getting double scoops of gelato afterward."

"Deal. And maybe we should get that anyway. You know, for luck."

"Right. Luck." I start my text message again.

Me: I'll talk to him.

Cole responds with praying hands, a heart, and a thumbs-up.

Audrey plants her hands on her hips. "No time like the present. I'm meeting Mema for yoga. Why don't you text Bryson? Maybe he can chat."

"I'm not sure I still have his number. I blocked it a long time ago."

"Ah."

She grabs my shoulders, turns me in the right direction, and gives me a shove. "Well, it sounds like you'll just have to drop in. And be nice! And ask him to help you with your homework!"

We part ways, and I drag my feet up the hill.

Why am I the one who has to baby him?

My mood sours further when I have to pass by my building supplies strewn around Mema's front yard to get to Bryson's house. I brought them all out a few days ago to see what else I need.

I need a builder.

Another thing that's not going my way.

Next to them, the plastic daises I brought to Mema's porch shiver in the breeze. She wasn't thrilled to have fake summertime flowers on her fall-themed porch, but she indulged me.

There's my reminder. So, where's my sunshine character? I can't seem to find her.

I trudge up Bryson's front steps, take a deep breath, and blow the loose hairs out of my face. For the fall festival. I force a smile and knock on the Dumars' front door.

"Come in. It's open!" Tyler calls from inside.

Um... okay. I push the door and step into the familiar living room. It doesn't look much different from how it did three years ago. Only this time, crayons claim every inch of the rug, and a Lego fortress is under construction on the coffee table. Bryson is perched on the edge of the couch, perusing an instruction book, while Tyler sits on the rug, attempting to force two bricks together.

I clear my throat. "Hey, guys."

Bryson glances up and does a double take. It's almost cartoonlike. His dark eyes go wide. His hair is wet, probably from his post-run shower.

Tyler scrambles to his feet and runs over, grinning ear to ear. "Emma!"

I muss his hair. "Hey, Tyler."

"Want to help us build the castle?"

"Sure." I avoid Bryson's gaze.

"Uncle Bryce is reading the instructions. He thinks we're missing pieces."

Bryson flips the book closed and taps it on his jeans. He gives me one of those half smirks that could mean "What's up?" or "Why are you here?" or maybe both.

My fingers fiddle with my jacket hem, and I force myself to meet his gaze. "Can we talk?"

He lifts a shoulder.

That wasn't a no.

Tyler starts stacking bricks again.

Bryson doesn't move, so I sit on the couch's other end.

The words *practically in love* seem to scream in the silence between us.

I clear my throat and set my camera bag next to me. "I wanted to say I'm sorry about what I said before, about us not being friends. That was…" I pause, searching for the right word. "Lame. And I'd like another shot at, you know, not being mortal enemies."

His smirk fades into something softer, more considering. That's a good sign, right?

Tyler drops his bricks and runs to the kitchen.

"And about the festival," I rush on. "I know you're avoiding me. But I don't want you to quit. It's in a couple of days, and we can make it through without letting the others down and without killing each other."

Tyler returns and offers me the cup he's holding with two hands. "It's water."

I take it and examine the purple cup and run my thumb over the white The Meeting House logo. "Hey, I remember this one."

"Yeah. Bryson and Nana said it was the one you always liked."

"Oh… thank you." They've been discussing me. And not necessarily in a bad way. I take a drink and smile at the kid.

He goes back to stacking bricks beside Bryson, whose ears have pinked.

"Anyway," I say. "We could still use your help. I could use your help."

"I'm not avoiding you."

I raise an eyebrow.

"Well, maybe a little."

Tyler tugs at Bryson's hand. "Uncle Bryce, you should help Emma."

"You think so?"

Tyler nods.

I set the cup on a coaster. "Hey, if you have a problem with me being there, I'll step aside. You'd be way better at organizing this thing than I am. I didn't want to do it in the first place."

"No. I don't want you to quit."

"You sure? I don't mind being lazy."

He rolls his eyes. "Yes. I'm sure."

"So, you'll stay in?"

"Yeah, I will. But only because Tyler wants me to." He musses Tyler's hair like I did.

Tyler jumps up. "Yay! Can I help?"

Bryson stands. "Sure. And you'll have to because Nana's not home. Isn't there a meeting in like ten minutes?"

The kid bounces on his toes. "Yay!"

"Yep." I get to my feet, pull the strap of my bag back over my head, and start for the door. I pause to look back. "Want to walk with me?"

Tyler rushes past me out the door. "I'm riding my bike."

We head out together, the Oklahoma wind returning to tunnel down the street after its very short absence. It's definitely getting cooler.

The silence stretches, but it's comfortable.

Things aren't exactly normal—I mean, we're not friends—but maybe less like enemies.

21

Bryson

Okay. So, Emma and I are trying this nonenemy thing again. And judging by the thick silence between us, it's really going well.

A gust of wind scatters leaves as we walk to the festival site, so I stuff my hands in my pockets. Next to me, she zips her coat and does the same. Tyler pedals ahead, not seeming to notice the chill.

Emma didn't say she wants to be friends—only that she wants to be nonenemies. Surely, we can handle that. Right?

But I'm still in the dark. I don't know why she's so mad at me after all this time. She said there's a lot I don't know, so why hasn't she told me?

"Emma—"

"Do you—"

We both start at the same time but cut off.

She chews her lip. "What were you going to say?"

"You first."

"Oh, I was thinking about our first fall break here. Do you remember?"

"Was that the one where Audrey was obsessed with getting what's-his-name to be her date to the dance?"

"That's the one. His name was Drew. She crushed on him for years after that. Honestly, she might still like him. My family kept coming here even after I stopped, so she's been around him every summer. He still texts her, which keeps her hopes up."

Her brow pinches, and she's quiet again. Is she thinking about why she stopped coming here? Will she tell me?

But she shakes her head, clearing away the dark cloud of the past. "And the hay fort! Remember?"

"How could I forget? It was epic. I told Cole about it, but he didn't think it would be in the budget. Maybe that's why they never did it again."

"Tyler would love it."

"Yeah. Maybe next year."

I give Tyler a high five as he speeds past on his bike. He wobbles and nearly topples.

Emma laughs, and I cup a hand around my mouth, "Nice save, Tyler."

He gives a thumbs-up and wobbles again.

I chuckle, returning my hand to my pocket. "So what did you do on those summers when your family came back without you?"

She leads us off the boardwalk and onto the sidewalk. "Summer camp. I was a camper until last summer when I became a counselor."

"I take it you like it there."

"Yeah. I do. It's my happy place."

"I remember when you used to say that about Carlton Landing."

Oops. Probably not the best thing to bring up. But everything about us, every shared memory, is from back then. How do I avoid it? But then again, *she* found a way to avoid it for the last three years.

She shoves the hair swirling around her face behind her ears. "Yeah. But sometimes things change."

They certainly do.

She jumps to another subject—again. "Oh, remember my cousin Hudson trying to teach us to dance? He wanted to make Audrey feel better after Drew turned her down."

"I seem to remember I was the only one of us who was any good."

She slaps my arm. "You were not!"

I cut my gaze to her.

"I mean, okay, fine. I was terrible. But I was twelve. I like to think I've picked up some rhythm since then." She steps onto the curb, walking along it like a balance beam. "I danced at Hudson's wedding. Well... some.

163

Once. Okay, one dance with Will. And that was before he ran off to find Morgan."

"One dance *with your cousin* at a wedding doesn't prove to me you're any good."

She attempts a scowl but only succeeds in barely suppressing a smile.

I start to say "you'll need to prove it at the dance," but that's probably taking it too far.

Finally, she laughs. "Fair point."

I have to look away. She's so beautiful.

Stop thinking about that.

She's just my pretty nonfriend / nonenemy. Someone I had a crush on once—past tense.

We round the corner, and I halt, putting a hand on her arm.

She follows my gaze and sucks in a breath. "Is that what I think it is?"

Cole sights us and hops onto a hay bale. One of many. He spreads his arms. "Ta-da!"

Emma and I jog over as the scent of hay and earth fills our senses.

Behind Cole towers a haphazard pyramid of rectangular hay bales. Tyler has already climbed on top.

I step onto one. "Please tell me we're making a fort."

"You bet. But, uh, these things are heavier than I thought."

Emma claps, tugs her camera from her bag, and snaps shots of Tyler. "This is awesome."

I jump over, closer to Cole. "I thought you said it wasn't in the budget."

"We made it work." He points toward a tractor up the hill as it maneuvers a larger round bale from a flatbed trailer. "We're renting from the farmer until Sunday, and we only have him and his tractor for another hour. We need to design this thing and have him position the bales now."

Emma's already stowed the camera, retrieved her notebook, and is thumbing through it to find a blank page. She starts sketching out a plan. "We need to move it farther from the pavilion."

"Agreed," says Cole. "We want it to be away from that and the stage."

Emma nods along. "Yep. And do you think we need more people?"

"That would be nice."

"I'll text Audrey and the others."

Cole tosses me a pair of work gloves, and we get started.

An hour later, the farmer has left, Will blasts country music from his portable speaker, and an epic hay fort is almost complete.

Tyler is loving every minute. Lucky kid. He couldn't lift a hay bale if he wanted to. He's alternated between zipping around on his bike and climbing on new haystacks.

Cole and I walk toward his truck to grab water bottles. He stretches his arms over his head. "I'll be sore tomorrow."

I pry the gloves from my aching fingers. "Me too. This is more difficult than I thought it would be. Hey, maybe *this* is why they never had the hay fort again."

"I believe it. So… what's up with you? First, you say you're out on the fall festival, and now you're here. What changed?"

Unbidden, my gaze darts to where Emma and Olivia are measuring the opening of the fort entrance.

He follows my gaze. "Ah, I figured as much."

My lips turn down. Am I so obvious? "It's not about her."

"You're still telling yourself that?" He tosses me a water. "So, you're friends again?"

"I… don't think so. I… don't know what we are. She told me she didn't want to be friends, so I decided to keep my distance, especially while she's interested in Kip."

Cole chuckles. "Yeah, I figured it was about him too."

"It's not. Anyway, then she comes to my house and talks me into coming out here today." I take a long drink. "She's so confusing. It's probably because she knew you needed extra people to build this thing."

"She didn't know I was doing this. It was a surprise."

I shed my jacket and let the breeze cool my body and my annoyance. New subject. "Somehow, your big surprise turned into a lot of extra work."

He makes a face, wiping sweat from it with his forearm. "Yeah. Sorry. It's looking good, though, right?"

"Definitely."

We walk back over, both carrying water bottles for the others. I head toward Morgan, Will, and Audrey, but he crosses in front of me. "Oh no, you don't. Take yours to Emma and Olivia."

"But—"

"The committee head has spoken."

"Okay, calm down. You're not the mayor."

"Not yet."

He veers away, and I duck into the fort entrance where Emma smiles my way.

Wow. No scowl. Maybe things are looking up.

Olivia brightens too. "Oh, thank you, thank you. I'm so thirsty."

She takes it, and I hold the other out to Emma. "How about you?"

She pulls it from my fingers, her hand brushing mine. "Thanks."

I look around so I don't stare as Emma quenches her thirst. "It's looking good over here."

"Thanks." Olivia wipes her mouth with the back of her hand.

"Olivia, can you help me with something?" Audrey waves her over, leaving me and Emma inside the fort.

She twists the cap back on her water bottle and sits on a square bale, acting as a step up to the next level. "Doesn't this feel like it did before? The weather, the smell. We spent so much time in that hay fort. We were all so sad to leave at the end of the break."

I sit across from her. "I hoped it would still be there when we returned for Christmas."

"Yeah, me too."

"And I remember destroying a few apples on that tree over there." I point at a nearby sugar maple covered in brilliant yellow leaves.

She giggles and places a hand over her chest. "That was in honor of my sister and her bruised heart."

"You swiped the apples from the bobbing tank, and I nabbed a slingshot from another booth."

"We launched them with Audrey and pretended the tree was Drew."

I rub my hands on my knees. "So violent."

She laughs and hauls her feet up on the hay bale, hugging her knees. "That was fun."

It was fun. And I was completely enamored with her, this girl who climbed on hay bales and swiped apples to make her sister feel better. This girl who raced me on our bikes and stuffed herself with pumpkin muffins. This girl who offered her friendship and smiles. I was a goner for that girl. Twelve years old and harboring a secret, round-bale-sized crush.

And that crush stayed with me for ages. But I never told her when it mattered. Leave it to me to blurt that secret years later during a fight.

I lean down and brace my elbows on my knees, studying my fingers. "Yeah. Those were the days."

The breeze rustles her hair around her face, and she pushes it over her shoulder. "They shut us down pretty quickly, though. You know, when they noticed the apples were disappearing. And then I got in trouble for stealing and being wasteful. Guilty on both counts, I suppose."

"I'd left to get more when you and Audrey were caught. You never told them I was helping."

She holds my gaze. Water bottle halfway to her lips. "No, I didn't."

But I did. Years later, when it mattered more. I told on her. But it was so long ago. What's she not telling me?

I open my mouth to ask, but Audrey shuffles into the fort, dragging a green play-scape slide. "Ready to attach the slide?"

Emma stands and helps her move it into position, but Audrey digs into her jacket pocket. "I have a text. Hold on." Her face falls when she swipes on the screen. "It's Drew. Again."

Emma tilts the phone her way. "So he knows you have a crush on him. He has a girlfriend. And he's still texting you?"

"Looks like it."

"Ignore him. Please."

Audrey nods and slides her phone back into her pocket, but her carefree mood has evaporated.

We position the slide, and Emma and I hold it on either side while Audrey adjusts the bracket that will keep it in place. Emma meets my gaze over the green plastic and then cocks her head. "Can you help her without me for a minute? I have an idea."

"Sure."

Her eyes are bright as she shifts the weight to me. "I'll be back."

And then she's running out of the fort and across the green toward home. She crosses the street and veers out of sight.

When I turn away, Audrey is grinning. "This feels like old times, huh?"

"Maybe too much."

"Hmm."

She positions the bracket. "I, uh, have a favor to ask."

"Yeah? What do you need?"

She tells me as she hammers the mallet, and we agree to text about it tomorrow.

We finish the slide as Emma comes rushing back around the corner carrying a grocery bag.

Tyler follows her in on his bike. "What's that?"

"You'll see." She yells at Will to play a specific song.

Her plan clicks into place the second she drops the bag in front of Audrey. I laugh.

"What? What is it?" Audrey asks.

Everyone gathers inside the fort, and Emma picks up a badly bruised apple from the bag. "I've assembled you for battle." She sounds much like she did six years ago. "One of us is under attack by the enemy. Drew Dobson from the land of Tulsa will not stop texting my sister even after he got a girlfriend. Time to launch this rotten fruit at the maple—also known as Drew."

Audrey rolls her eyes. "Are you serious?"

Emma puts a hand on her hip and tosses the apple up and down with the other. "Do I look like I'm joking? Come on. For old times' sake. And I'm certain it will make you feel better." She bends and wriggles a slingshot from her bag.

"That won't get it to the maple tree," Will says.

"Hush. Let her give it a try."

Audrey shakes her head and takes the items. She's smiling as she lets it fly. It lands right over the hay wall, yards away from the tree.

Emma scratches her cheek. "Uh, maybe just throw it. Oh, and there are only two more. Mema wouldn't let me take the good ones."

Will turns up the song. "The pressure is on."

Audrey throws the apple and barely misses the trunk.

We groan and then offer encouraging words.

Emma hands her the last apple, the mushiest one. "This is the one, Audrey. You can do it. Time to let him go."

Hmm. Is this some Blackwell sister ritual? Did they throw rotten fruit at me after I supposedly wronged Emma?

The music blares. Almost like slow motion, Audrey rears back and launches the apple.

It arcs over the hay and splats against the sugar maple.

We cheer, giving the moment much more enthusiasm than warranted. Emma hugs Audrey as they jump around. Then Morgan scoops a pile of leaves and throws them into the air. They swirl around the girls.

Emma grabs her camera and snaps shot after shot, and before we know it, she's ushered us outside the fort where the low sun bathes us in golden light.

Tyler climbs up on the wall and spreads his arms wide. "Emma! Look, it's the golden hour."

She clicks away in his direction. "That's right. And what does that mean?"

He jumps down, arms flailing. "It's the perfect time to take photos. Can I try?"

"Sure. Come stand over here."

I sit on a bale out of the way. "Be careful, Tyler. Her camera is expensive."

"I will, Uncle Bryce."

With Emma's help, Tyler takes candid shots of the others as they reenact Audrey's triumph and a couple shot of Morgan and Will.

Eventually, he turns the lens my way. "Can I take one of Uncle Bryce?"

Emma's dancing gaze lands on me. Her lips turn up at the corners. "Of course." She gets down on Tyler's level. "He's in the perfect spot. See how the sunlight behind him makes his hair kind of glow?"

I shift. "Oh, that's okay. She doesn't need any of me."

Tyler starts clicking away. "Be still, please."

There's nothing for me to do but sit here awkwardly.

Emma's grin grows. "Smile, Uncle Bryce."

I shake my head and show some teeth.

Tyler gives Emma a push. "Let me take one of you guys."

"Oh, that's okay."

"Please?"

Emma's gaze bounces between Tyler and me. "Um. I don't—"

"Pleeease." Tyler pushes his lip out.

She ruffles his hair. "Okay, fine."

She walks toward me and shrugs.

The wind sends her hair flying around her rosy cheeks. Her smile is soft and timid. My heart ticks up a beat, still enamored.

She sits next to me, close but not touching, and clears her throat.

Tyler lifts the camera. "Say cheese."

A gust of wind sends sumptuous yellow leaves flying. Emma laughs, and I smile and turn her way. Tyler clicks away.

Fly away leaves. Fly. And take my wasted heart with you.

As much as I warn myself away from this girl, my heart won't listen.

Yep, I'm still a goner.

"Emma," Olivia calls from under the tree. "Look who's here."

We follow her gaze to where Kip is getting out of his truck near the pavilion.

Right. Reality check.
Pull it together, Bryson.
Nonfriend. Nonenemy. That's all.
And that's fine.

22

Emma

Bryson and I smile for one more photo, and then Tyler, whose attention has moved on to a couple of kids riding their bikes, starts to set my camera on the ground. Bryson rushes to him and takes it.

Tyler runs off, and Bryson holds it out to me, his smile not quite reaching his eyes anymore. "That was close."

"Thanks. Good thing you're fast."

"I had a feeling something like that might happen."

He watches me with those beautiful dark eyes, and I'm thrown off-balance again.

He was in love with me?

The statement hovers every time I'm around him.

My lips twitch to ask him to look through our photos together.

"Emma!" Olivia motions me over, nodding in Kip's direction in a way that's meant to be discreet but most definitely is not.

"Just a sec," I call over the wind.

Bryson hands me my bag, not meeting my eye, and veers in the other direction. A pang zips through my chest.

I grip my camera, mesmerized by how the golden sun reflects off his hair, giving it a reddish hue. I snap one last photo and then secure the lens cap.

Audrey ducks out of the fort and slides in beside me. She hooks her thumbs in her pockets, facing Bryson's retreating form. "Get any good shots?"

"Uh, yeah. I got some great ones. Plenty for the festival committee and my Instagram account."

"Any good ones of Bryson?"

"Yeah, they're okay."

"Um-hmm. Can I make an observation?"

I should say no. I sling the strap over my head. "Sure. Why not?"

"You like him. You don't want to. But you do."

"I do not. I'm a team player. That's all."

"I bet you're dying to look at those photos."

"I'm excited to look at all of them."

"Okay."

Olivia flails her arms. "Emma, come here. This might be your chance."

I nod, and Audrey straightens a hay bale. "Do you even like your McDarcy anymore?"

I back away from her in Olivia's direction. "Of course I do. I mean, look at him."

She can't argue with me there. Kip has shed his jacket even though it's chilly out.

"Yeah, but he's not the kind of guy you normally go for. Does he even like to read?"

The muscles in my jaw clench as my eyes narrow. "That's the point, Audrey. I'm trying something different. I'm getting out of my comfort zone." I plaster on a smile. "I'm sunshine."

"Maybe you should just be yourself."

"I am. I'm myself. Don't worry."

"Okay, whatever you say."

I head over to Olivia, leaving my sister and her observations behind.

"Finally." Olivia smirks and pulls me by the arm. "Look, Kip is all alone. You should go over there. Strike up a conversation. Ask him to build that library."

"What makes you think he'll say yes this time?"

"Well, he never said no."

"True."

With a clang, Kip throws something in the back of his truck and then heads toward the driver's door.

"Uh-oh." Olivia nudges me in his direction. "Better hurry."

Kip climbs in, cranks the engine, and peels out.

His taillights fade into the distance, and Olivia pats my shoulder. "Well. Maybe next time."

"Yeah, maybe."

Or maybe not.

***

The next day, I walk to Coffee Connection in the wee hours to start the early shift with one of the other employees. After the morning rush, I have minutes to spare, so I make a double latte and visit my beloved books in the back hallway.

"Hey, friends," I whisper as I run my fingers over their spines. I can't wait to get them in a more prominent location. Does anyone even know they're here?

I dust them off and then press my lips together. Someone has placed unopened bags of coffee on my shelf. I shove them in the too-full space above where they should be.

"There, that's better."

The shift passes, and I don't even watch for Kip… much. He's in and out, likely working at both the house and the stage today. He's so busy. Will he ever have time for the library?

After work, I spend the afternoon setting up a photo booth near the pavilion using the spare hay bales. When the pumpkins arrive, I'll finish it out.

Following dinner with Mema, I grab my laptop and return to Coffee Connection, intent on doing my homework. Audrey insists on coming with me, even though she's on fall break and has no work to do. I suspect she's tagging along to ensure I don't get distracted by my manuscript... or anything else.

Olivia is working the evening shift, so after ordering our drinks from her, we sit at my usual table by the window.

Audrey takes the seat facing the house next door. "Don't want you getting distracted by anything over there."

I roll my eyes. "He doesn't work past five anyway."

Her phone vibrates with a text, so while she's intent on that, I flip my laptop open and read through the instructions again.

And I get stuck again.

Several failed attempts later, I give up and rest my forehead on the table. "I'll never graduate."

Audrey sets her phone on the table. "Yes, you will. You can do this."

The door dings, but I don't move. "No, never. I'll be the eternal high schooler. That's what they'll call me. Everyone will keep moving on without me." I knock my head against the wooden surface.

"Um, need some help?" a familiar voice asks.

I sit up so fast I rattle my latte, splashing it onto the saucer.

Bryson chuckles and clatters out a chair between Audrey and me at the small table.

I snap my mouth closed and give her a look, but she won't meet my eye. She picks up her phone.

I rub my forehead. There's probably a red mark. "What are you doing?"

"Not much. Came for a coffee. And to work on some programming homework."

"You don't have a programming class."

"No. I don't."

I round on Audrey. "You asked him to help me?"

"Who me? I would never."

A mortified lump forms in my throat.

"I don't need your help. Either of you."

"Emma, you're failing. Bryson can help you."

"Audrey, I told you that in confidence."

"Just let him look at it."

I tug my laptop toward me. "No." I send her a pleading look.

Bryson taps the table and then stands. "I'm going to order and sit at the coffee bar." He meets my gaze. "Let me know if you want me to come back over."

He moves away, and I lean toward Audrey. "This is humiliating. It's bad enough I accidentally didn't graduate. Now I can't even complete my assignments for my last class, the only one standing between me and a diploma."

"You would let your pride keep you from accepting his help?"

"It's not pride."

"Yes, it is. Now swallow it."

I duck my chin. "I told him the class was going fine."

"Well, this is what you get for lying."

He always had better grades than me. "He's so smart. It's embarrassing."

"Well, he knows the truth now, so you might as well use him."

I glare at my clenched fingers.

"Look, he wants to help you. Maybe he wants to do it to make amends for what happened between you. Let him."

My arms fall to my side, and I release a slow breath. "Fine."

Bryson sits at the coffee bar across from Olivia. He must feel my gaze because he turns his head, and those deep-brown eyes pierce me again. One corner of his mouth lifts.

I swallow. "Bryson."

The smile grows into a grin. "Yes?"

Practically in love.

See, this is why I shouldn't be around him.

"Will you help me?"

Audrey kicks my foot. "Say, please."

I glare at her. "Please."

***

Two hours later, Audrey has gone home, and I'm the one smiling because I finally get it. I actually get my homework.

And it's all thanks to Bryson.

He's still here, seeing it through to the bitter end.

I tilt my cup to let the last drops of my cold coffee trickle into my mouth. "Thank you for helping me. Really. I couldn't have done this without you."

He shakes his head. "You're welcome, and do you want me to get you another coffee?"

"Nope. Can't have too much caffeine before bed."

With the weight lifted from my shoulders, I can't stop grinning.

Embarrassed one minute. Frustrated the next. And now, happy.

He probably thinks I'm insane.

I post my work to my class website and hit send as my boss comes over. "Hey, guys. We're closing in five. And, Emma, can I talk to you before you leave?"

My eyebrows pull together. "Sure. Let me grab my stuff."

Joanna walks away, and I stow my laptop in my backpack.

Bryson stands and shoves his hands in his hoodie pockets. "Well, I'm headed home."

"No jacket?"

"Nah."

"Don't freeze. And thanks again."

"No problem."

He starts to say something else, but Joanna calls me over.

He waves and heads for the door, glancing back before exiting.

I approach the coffee bar where Joanna is closing the register and Olivia's restocking the mugs. "Hey, is everything okay?"

Joanna tosses a towel over her shoulder. "Emma, I'm so sorry, but I need the space in the back hall for inventory. It's too crowded back there, and I have some Christmas merchandise coming soon."

Oh. My shoulders droop. "Yeah, okay. Do you want me to take the books now?"

"No, no. By Sunday is fine, okay?"

"Yeah, no problem."

Olivia walks me out. "Sorry, you have to move your books. Maybe your predicament will persuade Kip to help you. They're almost done with the stage and the house next door. I'm sure he'll be free after that."

I straighten. "Yeah, you're right."

It's time to ask him again. I need the library now more than ever.

23

Emma

On Wednesday, we're only two days out from the festival, and the tasks have started piling up. Cole is on edge, having checked the weather about a million times, but he's deemed it safe to start arranging some of the sturdier decorations in the pavilion and across the lawn.

The pumpkins arrived, so I finished decorating the photo booth—which turned out beautifully—and I've also been snapping photos along the way. Mr. Johnston, the festival chair, has been using them to create hype on the Carlton Landing social accounts.

The stage is complete, and only the steps leading up to it remain. Kip is bent over them, muscles flexing under his snug T-shirt as he hammers away. Over the last few days, he and his dad have worked countless extra hours to wrap up their work projects.

"Earth to Emma. I'm ready," Olivia says from atop a ladder. She smirks when I look up at her. "And stop staring and go over there and ask Mr. Tall, Dark, and Handy about your library. And maybe ask him out while you're at it."

I toss up the end of the twinkle lights we're stringing overhead. "I'm not asking him out, and I wasn't staring. I was admiring the stage."

"Sure you were."

Actually, I was. "Besides, every time I try to bring up the library, it's a disaster."

"Well, he's finally warming up to all of us. Want me to put in a good word for you?"

"No! I'm fine. I just want to hire him to build the library."

"Okay, okay. But you are not a quitter, Emma Blackwell. Your McDarcy and your novel inspiration await." She cranes her neck in his direction. "And look, he's eating his lunch all alone. Get your cute butt over there and ask him."

Olivia's love for matchmaking excited me two weeks ago. Now, I'm not sure about any of it. But I would like someone who knows what they're doing to build my library. "Okay. Fine. I'll ask about the library."

Olivia squeals, bouncing too much for someone standing on a ladder. "Whoa."

I grab a rung. "Calm yourself. Let's not break a leg today."

"Okay, Okay. I'm good. Now, go. I'll finish this strand."

"Fine." I square my shoulders. "Wish me luck."

"Break a leg."

I glare over my shoulder. "No. No broken legs."

"Right."

I walk over and try to keep from fidgeting. Kip's legs dangle over the stage as he eats a sandwich from a brown paper bag. With earbuds in, he kicks his foot to a beat I can't hear.

"Hey, Kip." I come near. He doesn't look up, so I repeat myself, louder this time.

He glances my way and pulls a bud from his ear. "What's up?"

I gesture toward the platform. "The stage looks good."

"Thanks." He takes a bite of his sandwich.

Okay. Moving on.

"So, about my library project—the one I've been bugging you about? I was wondering if you'd thought about it anymore."

In the awkward pause, he finishes chewing. He scratches the back of his neck. "Nah, I haven't had the chance. I'll say maybe for now. Need to get through this project." He shrugs and pats the stage.

Not a yes. Not a no. Once again, his response is about as clear as Lake Eufaula. That is to say, not clear at all.

Super.

"Okay, thanks." I turn away, and Audrey waves from across the street. She's walking toward me, a tray of coffee in hand. I make my way to her.

"I got you a present," she says.

"Oh, bless you. I just got put in the maybe zone by Kip again."

She frowns and hands me a cup. "Did Olivia finally talk you into asking him out, or did you ask him about the library."

I nearly spit the hot liquid out. "The library. There's no telling what he'd say if I asked him out."

"He'd probably say the same thing." She pitches her voice low. "*Maybe.*" She rolls her eyes. "Emma. I have to tell you something."

"What?"

"I don't think he'll ever build the library for you. Or be your romance inspiration."

I cross my arms. "Ouch."

"Sorry."

"Oh, who am I kidding? Maybe you're right. After all, I do always go for the wrong guy."

She rubs my arm. "Nah. Maybe you just haven't met the right guy yet." She spins away to deliver more coffee, but I don't miss her say. "Or maybe you have."

24

Bryson

An annoyingly upbeat song lights up my phone. It vibrates on my bedside table. Better not hit the snooze button for a third time if I intend to get my jog in. The festival kicks off today, and there's a lot to do.

I tug on my running shoes and hit the streets. The sun is already peeking over the treetops around Carlton Landing, and the air has a crisp bite, the kind that wakes you up better than one of Olivia's double-shot espressos. My feet pound between rows of vibrant red and orange trees. It's just me and my shadow stretching long on the pavement.

I jog along a path near the lake, taking in the serene setting and letting it calm me. Another runner waves as we pass. By the time Coffee Connection comes into view, I feel good about the day.

As I run by, Emma pushes through the door to bring a steaming mug out to a patron braving the crisp morning on the porch. She doesn't even frown at me.

Yep, it's going to be a good day.

Back at home, I transition from sweaty jogger to presentable human and settle at the kitchen table to get some schoolwork done. Mom's pretty much left the responsibility of getting work done up to me since it's my last year of high school, and I admit I'm about a week behind in my curriculum plan. I've been distracted by the festival... and other things.

After lunch, I head to the festival grounds to meet with the committee and find out what Cole needs from us today. His mouth is tight as he frowns at his clipboard. The stress might be getting to him.

I peek at his scrawled list. "What's wrong?"

He glances up, startled. "Oh, hey, Bryson. I'm...just not sure." He taps a knuckle on the paper. "I feel like I'm forgetting things. But I don't know what. I don't know what I don't know. I've never done this before."

I clap him on the shoulder. "It'll be fine. Everyone will have a great time."

Others from other committees are scattered about. The decorating committee is out in full force today.

Olivia spins in a circle, arms out. "This place looks amazing!"

Beside her, Emma snaps photos. She meets my gaze. My heart does a little skip.

Olivia tosses the end of her scarf over her shoulder. "I have bad news about the ice."

Cole hugs his clipboard. "Okay. Let's hear it."

"The corner store doesn't keep bags of ice in the offseason."

Cole lets out a long breath. "And we were counting on them to fill the soda coolers. Can anyone run to town and get some?"

"I need to finish setting up the face-painting booth," Olivia says. "Besides, won't most people drink coffee or hot chocolate?"

"Yeah, but we also have soda, and we want it to be chilled, right?"

Emma moves next to me. "Maybe Bryson and I could go get it. We don't need to set up our games until tomorrow morning anyway."

I still. Really? And I need to fix whatever expression has crossed my face because she adds, "I mean, if you want to."

I stuff my hands in my pockets and go for normal. "Yeah. Sure. There's plenty of time."

Cole lets out a breath. "Great. That'd be awesome. Maybe get enough for today and tomorrow while you're at it. We'll store it in the extra coolers. And keep the receipt."

A golden leaf floats onto Emma's shoulder, and she brushes it away. "No problem."

Cole and Olivia rush off to their next task. Emma's long hair blows in the crisp breeze, and the chill pinks her cheeks. I look away.

Nonenemies. Nonfriends.

"I can drive if you like." I nod toward home. "We can take my dad's truck."

"Sure. It's for the best. I might've forgotten how since I haven't left Carlton Landing since I got here."

"Really? You haven't?"

She shakes her head as we make our way to my house. "Haven't had anywhere to go. All my friends are off at college meeting new people."

"What about Olivia? She lives in Eufaula, right?"

"She's here pretty much every day. No need to leave to see her."

I kick at a rock. "That's how I've felt every time we've moved over the last three years—like any new friends I made were moving on without me. Again and again. It can be pretty lonely."

"Yeah. It can. Sorry you had to move so much."

"It's all right. I'm used to it by now. Mom says we might stay here at least until summer. So, hopefully, the next time I move, it will be where I want to go."

We reach my house, and I run in to tell Mom where I'm going and grab the keys.

The corner of her mouth twitches. "Just you and Emma?"

I rush out, not wanting to answer any questions. "Yep."

Emma and I climb in Dad's brand-new Ford and head out of Carlton Landing.

She sets her camera bag on the seat between us and adjusts the heater to blow her way. "What was that station our parents used to love to listen to?"

"Um, I know what you're talking about, but I can't remember. Try scanning, and we'll see if we can find it."

She pauses on an old country song. I'm not sure if it's the right station, but it fits the mood.

We fall into silence until I can't stand it any longer. "Nice weather for the festival." I'm aiming for light and casual but likely hitting somewhere closer to awkward and desperate. The weather? Really?

"Definitely." Her gaze is fixed on the passing scenery. "The leaves are beautiful this time of year."

"Yep." At least, we've tiptoed past my weather blunder.

But what now? Shouldn't we get some stuff out in the open now that we have a chance to talk?

"Emma," I say—and regret it.

"Hmm?" She's still gazing out the window.

"Never mind."

She stops me with that green-eyed gaze.

Focus on the road, buddy. "I don't know. I was thinking maybe we should talk. About...everything."

When I peek back, her eyes are wide. She opens her mouth. Nothing comes out.

I grip the steering wheel. "I'll go first. Okay?"

At her silence, I plunge on. "You were right. I was jealous. I hated seeing you with him. I'm not saying it was okay. But that's how I felt."

I coast into a gas station, parking near the ice bin. I keep my eyes forward and let the engine idle. "When Eric told me you guys were going to climb the water tower, I was scared for you. I mean, I knew you were scared of heights. That was so dangerous, Emma."

She pulls a lock of hair over her shoulder. "I know. But to be fair, I didn't know he wanted to climb it. He didn't tell me. Also, I wanted you to come. Don't you remember me asking you? Right before we left?"

I cut my gaze in her direction. "Eric told me he didn't want me to come."

Her eyebrows shoot high.

"It's true. He was always telling us different things. Pitting us against each other. Anyway, I was afraid for you. I didn't want you to—die or something."

A man and his son exit the station, and I rub my face. "After it was over and I realized you really didn't want to ever talk to me again, I was... confused. I was devastated. I'd lost you as a friend, and I can't tell you how many times I've wished I could go back in time and take back that day. I didn't even get to tell you I was sorry. I sent so many texts and tried calling. I even had my mom call your mom, but she said you refused to talk to me. I felt... desperate. I didn't have many friends because of all the moving. You were like the only constant friend."

A bitter laugh slips out. "Did you know I even got online and bought a bus ticket to Oklahoma?"

Emma swings her gaze my way as she threads her hair between her fingers. "You did?"

"Yeah. But, of course, my parents found out. After that, we talked a lot about letting go. Moving on. And, eventually, I did."

We're silent now.

"I was so mad, Bryson."

"I know. Are you still?"

"Not usually." She picks at her jacket cuff. "But… sometimes."

I nod. "Do you still talk to Eric?"

Again, those perfect eyebrows go up. "No. I never saw him or talked to him again after that. I blocked his number too."

"Really?"

"Yes. Really." She laughs bitterly. "You still think I liked him? That I wanted to date him?"

I open my mouth, but nothing comes out.

She lifts her palms. "Bryson, I didn't like him like that. I never did." She scoffs and turns her head toward the ice bin. "We were all so clueless."

Before I can respond to this, she opens her door and slides out. "Come on. Ice to buy."

I follow her in, but I'm missing something.

25

Emma

The ice rattling in Bryson's truck bed is like a
metronome, ticking off the awkward silence between
us. I pretend I'm interested in the passing fields, but my
hands are knotted together in my lap. I might need a
crowbar to separate them.

To keep him from bringing up things I don't want to
talk about, I wave back down the road. "Did you know
that gas station is where Morgan and Will first met?"

"Really?"

"Yeah. I heard it was pretty messy. Avoid the ICEE
machine. And the coffee, for that matter."

"Noted." He drums his thumbs on the steering
wheel. We spiral back into silence as our parents'

favorite nineties country station twangs through the speakers.

"So," he says after a minute. "Will you tell me your side of the story?"

I suck in a deep breath. That's when the water tower looms into view, tall and mocking against the Oklahoma sky. My stomach nose-dives.

"Emma? Please." His tone soft, he follows my gaze. "Ah."

He doesn't get it. And there's only one way he ever will.

"Fine." Another opportunity like this may not come. It's time. I nod toward the tower. "That water tower represents the worst day of my life. When I see it, it makes me think of betrayal—and not just from you—and think of the police, eternal embarrassment, being punished, and lots more."

"Okay. Tell me what happened."

"That night, I said yes when Eric told me he wanted to sneak out and go to town. I don't know what got into me. You know I wasn't a bad kid. I suppose I felt like doing something crazy. Something different. I was frustrated with you for not joining us, and I was already mad at you for other stuff."

"Like what?"

Clueless. I roll my eyes. "That's another story. I'll stick to this one. So Eric claimed his car was out of gas. And maybe it was. I don't know. He talked me into taking my mom's car, which was a mistake. I only had a permit, so he drove. I knew he wanted to hang out at the water tower. But I had no idea he planned to climb it. When we arrived, he put on a backpack I didn't even know he'd brought. He started climbing and told me to follow. I didn't want to, but of course, he called me chicken. Plus, it was dark. I didn't want to be left alone down there. So I started climbing. Sloooowly."

I can almost feel the cool metal under my palms, the height making my head spin.

"He'd already been at the top for a while before I even got halfway. I'd already decided I wasn't going all the way to the top when I saw the police lights in the distance."

Bryson makes a face.

"Eric saw them too and started climbing back down. He moved so fast he passed me. It was much scarier going down than up. When he got to the bottom, he yelled at me to hurry. By then, I was scared to death and lightheaded. He got mad, which didn't help me go any faster. Then he yelled up that he was out. He dropped the backpack and took off on foot."

"He left you?"

"Yeah."

With the water tower behind us, we cruise across the Highway 9 bridge over Lake Eufaula. The sun sparkles on the water, and I gaze at it.

"He left the next morning. His grandma said he decided to spend the rest of the summer with his aunt. I never saw him again."

"You really never saw him again?"

"Nope. Never."

A muscle ticks in his jaw. "What happened once the cops arrived?"

"They had to talk me down the last twenty-five feet. And that's when the real trouble started. They searched Eric's bag and found a handful of spray paint cans. I swore it wasn't mine, but they didn't believe me. They thought I'd dropped it down ahead of me. It turns out Eric had spray-painted every inch of space he could reach on the water tower, though we couldn't see the extent of the damage until the next morning. The city had painted it earlier that spring—they'd had some trouble with paint vandalism around town over the last few months. Maybe it was Eric. Maybe it wasn't. Who knows? But they thought it was me."

We turn onto the long drive leading down to Carlton Landing.

Bryson grips the steering wheel so tight his fingers are white. "Then what?"

"Well, they saw I was in my mom's car and didn't have a driver's license. They let me call my parents and drove me to the police station. I can't even explain how angry Mom and Dad were. In the end, my parents believed me, but the police weren't sure what to believe. The city was ready to crack down hard on a vandal. I was charged with vandalism, and a court date was set."

We pull into a parking spot near the festival site, and Bryson cuts the engine. Neither of us get out.

He swallows, not meeting my eye. "And were you convicted?"

I stare at the hay fort. It's already crawling with happy kids. "No. But we worked out a deal. As long as I paid for the damage and attended a juvenile diversion program—with actual juvenile delinquents, I might add —the charges would be dropped. So I did. It costs a lot to touch up the paint on a water tower, and, of course, I didn't have enough money to cover the cost, so my parents paid for it. I'm still on a payment plan to pay them back." I sigh. "Not to mention, I couldn't keep Lucy from talking about it at school or church. Juicy gossip to a twelve-year-old. Some must still wonder if I did it."

I finally glance his way.

His eyes are wide. "Emma. I—I had no idea."

I don't break eye contact. "I didn't know you were the one who told on us until the next morning."

"I'm—"

The passenger door wrenches open, and I'm face-to-face with Olivia, who's bouncing with energy. "I've been looking everywhere for you. I have huge news."

I don't move from the cab. "What is it?"

"I told him. I know you didn't want me to, but it seemed like the best way to get results, so I did. I told Kip you're interested in him."

I force myself not to look over at Bryson. "What?"

"Yeah. And guess what? He's totally into it!"

I gawk at her.

"What? It's what you've been wanting for weeks. He plans to ask you to be his date to the dance tomorrow." She claps and bounces on her toes.

"I can't believe it," is all I manage.

"Believe it, girl. Oh, and look. Here he comes."

Sure enough, Kip saunters over from across the field, dripping with confidence. It's like the end of the *Pride and Prejudice* movie when Darcy crosses the field to find Lizzie and declare his love. Only I don't feel like Lizzie. This is someone else's movie. "I don't know, Olivia. Maybe it's not the right time with everything that's going on."

"Are you kidding me? It's all you've talked about at work for the last month. Getting that meet-cute."

"The time for meet-cutes has passed."

"Maybe, but this could be totally fun and great inspiration for your novel." She winks. Kip is halfway to us now. "And you better say yes! You'll make me look like an idiot."

I squirm, and my seat creaks. Bryson's brow is drawn, and he's scowling at the spot where his fingers are still gripping the steering wheel. But when his gaze meets mine, his face softens, and he gives me his oh-so-beautiful half smile. That smile says, "I want you to be happy." "She's right. It's what you wanted. You might as well give it a chance."

"Right?" Olivia says.

Something inside me that had been building against my will over the last two weeks deflates. Bryson wants me to accept.

I open my mouth to say something when Kip appears at my open door. Olivia scrambles out of the way.

"Hey, Emma." Kip gives me his own beautiful smile, but somehow its effect falls flat. He drapes an arm over the door and barely acknowledges Bryson. "I was wondering if you wanted to go to the dance with me tomorrow night."

I hesitate, and Olivia gives me a dirty look. Her frown says, "What's wrong with you?"

Bryson nods, still wearing his be-happy smile.

Kip's dimple folds into his cheek.

Maybe I *should* go.

Bryson's not interested in me.

Not that I care.

I put my back to him and pick at my jacket cuff again. "Um. Sure. Okay."

"Yeah?"

"Yeah."

"Cool. I'll pick you up at seven." He lifts his palm. "Give me your phone, and I'll put my number in."

I hesitate at the demand but hand it over as another idea strikes me. "Maybe we can finally talk about my Little Free Library."

"Nah. I don't have time to do that. We were just hired for a project that starts on Monday." He shrugs and returns my phone. "Text me your address. I'll see you tomorrow."

He strolls away, but I don't feel the way I thought I would.

Olivia's right. I've been thinking about this forever.

So why am I not ecstatic?

But I already know why.

I look over at the boy who's wholly derailed me, but he's already turned away.

26

Emma

Bryson unlatches the truck door and slides from the seat. I open my mouth to call out to him, but I honestly don't know what to say. He didn't even say sorry when I told him about everything that happened three years ago.

I clamp my mouth shut as he moves to the back of the truck to haul ice into the hut beside the pavilion.

He'll have to find someone else to help him unload. I need to get out of here. I jog home, take the steps past sunny fake flowers two at a time, and barrel through Mema's front door like an Oklahoma twister. I barely register the familiar creak of the hardwood floor. Neither Mema nor the others are in the living room, so my feet carry me straight up the stairs into the bunk room and to the ladder leading to the quiet loft. I climb and emerge into my childhood. Everything is the same. The ceiling rises to a point above my head, and four beanbags circle the fluffy rug at my feet. This was my and my sisters' secret hideout.

I drop my camera bag to the floor and collapse onto one of the beanbags resting on the worn-out rug, the same one where Audrey, Bryson, and I plotted to sneak cookies or plan our next outing.

I fish my camera from the bag and torture myself by flipping through some recent photos. I start with the ones of Tyler atop the hay bales and move through the formation of the fort all the way to our golden-hour photo shoot. There's Cole, Olivia and Audrey, Morgan and Will, and finally, Bryson. My thumb slows its scroll. And then there's Bryson and me. The leaves float around us. I'm laughing. He's looking at me in a way that makes my heart hurt. I've ruined everything. The last photo from that day is of his back. Walking away from me.

I turn the camera off.

"Emma? You okay?" Audrey's voice echoes up the wood staircase. I say nothing, and soon, footsteps trudge their way up.

She creaks up the ladder until her head pops into view. Once she's seated across from me, she glances around the space. "Wow, so many memories."

"I know. Maybe too many."

Her searching gaze lands on me. "What's up, you?"

"Nothing."

"Right." She crosses her arms. "I'll sit here and stare at you until you tell me."

I grip my camera bag. "Fine. Kip asked me out."

"Ah." She smiles like she knew what this would do to me all along. She taps her chin. "And though it's what you said you wanted, it didn't feel like you thought it would?"

I tuck the camera away and sink further into my beanbag. Resting my head back, I close my eyes. "Pretty much."

"And so you turned Kip down. I doubt his ego will suffer for long."

I peek at her. "Um. Not exactly."

"What do you mean, not exactly?" She sits up straight. "You said yes?"

I cross my arms over my face to cover my eyes. "And right in front of Bryson."

"Oh. Uh. I need more details."

So I fill her in on everything, and by the time I unshield my eyes, she's fighting an astonishing smile.

"What? Is my misery amusing to you?"

"No. No. It's that I was right. Admit it. You like him. Bryson."

I groan. "I don't want to like him."

"Sure. Sure. And it's most inconvenient since you've sworn to loathe him for all of eternity."

The corner of my mouth turns up at the butchered Jane Austen quote.

"Admit it."

"Ugh. Yes. I like him." I stand and pace the room. "What am I supposed to do now? Olivia pushed me into saying yes to Kip right in front of him." I chew on my lower lip. "And now, it's like I'm stuck in one of my rom-coms, and I'm to the point in the book where I've sabotaged everything."

"First, I'm pretty sure all your novels have a happy ending."

"Of course. Sad endings suck. But this is real life."

She laughs. "And second, since when do you let Olivia—or anyone—script your life? It's not too late to get out of the date with Kip."

I plop back down. "I know."

She waits for me to say more, and when I don't, she leans forward, elbows on her knees. "What do you want, Emma? Is there a part of you still wanting a shot with Kip?"

"No."

"And you like Bryson. Do you think he likes you?"

"No. I don't know. Maybe."

"And, answer honestly. Have you forgiven him for the whole water-tower fiasco?"

"I don't know. It's hard to relinquish a grudge I've been carrying for three years. It's like asking me to give up coffee."

Audrey rolls her eyes. "Let's put your anger in perspective. Bryson wasn't the one who followed along with Eric's bonehead plan. Bryson didn't do anything illegal. He didn't climb that water tower. You did."

"Ouch."

"Tell me it's not true."

"Audrey, I was fifteen. I was stupid."

She throws up her hands. "So was he! He was just a kid like you were. He had no idea what would happen. He says he was afraid for your safety and was probably mad at you too. And, if I'm being honest, I'm glad someone stopped you from climbing any further. What if you fell? You're terrified of heights." She lifts her palms. "And Bryson knew that."

Audrey's speech cuts me down to about two inches tall. She's right. I'm the one who did something wrong. Not Bryson. Maybe it's not only time to forgive Bryson but also time to own up to my part in our broken friendship.

She crosses her legs in front of her. "You always say you go for the wrong guy. Maybe it's time to go for the right guy. Maybe you've missed what's in front of you all this time."

"What if he doesn't like me like that anymore?"

She shrugs. "If you turn down Kip, there's always the chance you'll end up with neither of them. But it might be worth the risk."

I nod and study my clenched fingers.

She stands and smooths out her skirt. "Think about it. Decide what you want and what you want to do about it. Either way, apologize to Bryson for your part in everything. It's the right thing to do." She steps toward the ladder. "And Mema made cookies. Should I grab some?"

I throw her a smile and my own *Pride and Prejudice* quote. "A thousand times yes."

She laughs and descends a few rungs. "And whatever happens, happens. You're author Emmie Blackwell. Go write your story." She finishes with a sweep of her arm.

I chuckle and give her a thumbs-up. "A bit dramatic. And maybe tomorrow."

"There's that sunshiny disposition I know and love!" She salutes and disappears.

Sunshine? I can't find it in me. And I'm tired of pretending to be something I'm not. I nestle into the beanbag and pull out my phone.

I start to swipe the screen open, but my fingers pause.

Wait. I'm not the sunshine character of this story. I'm the grouchy girl who blocked my best friend's phone number and held a three-year grudge. I'm not sunny Lizzy Bennet. I'm... Darcy.

I'm the grump in this grumpy-sunshine story.

Or maybe there's no sunshine at all. This is a friends to enemies to... what?... story.

I open my contacts and search for Bryson Dumar.

There, it is. It's been there all along.

I touch his name, and his number pops onto the screen.

No telling how many messages I missed. How many phone calls.

And I deliberately turned them away.
I let out a breath, and at long last, I tap Unblock.

27

Bryson

After finishing up with the ice, returning Dad's truck, and helping Cole with other last-minute necessities, I head home to change before the movie on the lawn. As I turn the corner onto Lower Greenway, Audrey steps off their porch.

She waves. "Hey, Bryson."

"Hey, Audrey. What are you up to?"

"I'm running out to snap a few photos of the movie night for Emma."

"You guys aren't going?"

"Morgan and Will are, but I'm staying in with Emma. I'm sure she'll pick an old rom-com we haven't seen in a while."

I palm the back of my neck. "So you've talked to her today?"

"Yeah. Sounds like you two had a heart-to-heart."

"I wouldn't call it that. But it did answer the question of why she's still holding a grudge." I rub that palm over my face. "I had no idea. I didn't know she got in so much trouble."

"I know. And I might have told you, but she made us all swear not to."

"But why wouldn't she talk to me? Yell at me, at least?"

She lifts a shoulder. "Who knows, Bryson? She was and is stubborn. She was embarrassed. Heartbroken."

"I tried to call her."

"I know. I'm sorry."

I wave up toward their second-story porch. "Playing games up there brought back a lot of memories. Good and bad."

She chuckles. "Nothing like two truths and a lie to make things awkward."

"If I recall, it was you who made things awkward. I never heard you say, which of your things was a lie?"

She grins, her teeth a white flash in the darkness. "None of them. They were all true. Emma's first book was self-published under a pen name. Unless she made it up, you guys did almost kiss on the porch once. But you would know better than me."

I kick at the pebbles beneath my feet. "Yeah, maybe. Almost."

"But then your girlfriend texted."

My gaze darts back to hers. "She wasn't my girlfriend. Just someone I was talking to."

She grins with too much understanding. "Whatever. And finally, yes, Emma always had a summer crush." The look on her face waits for me to put something together.

"Do you mean me?"

She rolls her eyes. "Clueless. Surely, you know she had a crush on you? She always did."

"No. I don't believe you. She always treated me like a friend."

"You always treated her like a friend. Even though I hear you recently confessed that you were 'practically in love' with her."

"Dude. Do you guys tell each other everything?"

"Yep."

"I still don't believe you."

Her finger taps her chin. "Wait here. I have an idea."

"What are you going to do?" I call after her as she runs up the front steps.

That finger moves to her lips. "Shh."

Is she about to embarrass me?

She's back in no time and creeps out the front door, hiding something in her jacket. She giggles, keeping her voice low. "I feel like I just swiped a book from the library's restricted section." She glances at the high loft window and then reveals a poorly designed book cover on a thin paperback. "And this book is definitely banned. Especially from you."

I take it, reading the title. *OK Summer Sun* by E. K. Black.

Emma Kate Blackwell.

I hold it up. "She wrote this?"

She nods. "She'll kill me if she knows I gave it to you. But you should read it. At least the first half. You inspired part of it."

"Me?"

"Yep. But, of course, your ending didn't make a good young adult romance, so she had to veer away around the midpoint."

I stare down at the book. "This... is about me and her?"

"Well, sort of. If we're getting technical, it's a fiction about two characters named Emily and Brant." She smiles again. "I better get going. Read it or don't. Either way, get it back into Mema's bookshelf sometime."

With that, she saunters away, leaving me holding a secret romance novel partially inspired by me.

Read it or don't.

I tap the book on my palm and then text Cole to tell him I can't make the movie tonight.

Um... yeah. I'm reading it.

28

Emma

"Emma, wake up." Audrey rips the blanket off my face.

She's already dressed and ready, and she's not even on a festival committee.

I groan and snug my covers back up.

The bed sags as she sits on the end and shakes my ankle. "It's already ten, and it's Fall Festival Day," she sings. "You have a job to do. And a date to break."

"Don't remind me."

She flips the blanket back again. "You've got this. You'll tell Kip you can't be his date tonight. You'll hang out with the little kiddies at the festival. And what about Bryson? What's your plan there?"

I sit up, wrapping my arms around my knees. "I don't know. Should I talk to him?"

"That sounds like a good place to start. Now get up. Lots to do."

She pats my head and saunters toward the door.

I throw a pillow. "Morning people are the worst."

It misses, and she blows me a kiss.

Forty-five minutes later, I step onto the porch and breathe in a lungful of crisp autumn air. What a glorious day. Chilly but not too cold. Perfect.

The sunny yellow of my fake daisies rests near my feet among Mema's deep-red, orange, and gold mums, real autumn flowers growing and thriving at the time they should. One golden mum was left unpotted because she ran out of space. It's so lonely by the front door still in the gardener's tray.

I set my camera bag on the ground and rip the plastic daisies from my flowerpot. I toss them aside to make a summertime craft with them in a few months. Then I carefully plant and water Mema's last mum and set it among the others.

No more fake sunshine.

It's time to put away last season's colors and make way for the current one's rich and beautiful hues.

I step back and snap a photo of my work as a gang of elementary kids races by on bicycles. Vibrant leaves chase them on the wind, and I click away in their direction too.

The corners of my lips turn up. It's Festival Day. Let's do this.

But first... coffee.

When I reach Coffee Connection and push through the door, Olivia waves. Ding. She's pouring beans into the espresso machine, so I close my eyes and take a deep breath. "My favorite smell in the world."

She laughs. "You've mentioned it. But wait, don't speak too soon." She turns on the grinder and pumps some into the portafilter. She holds it out toward me.

I climb onto a stool and inhale another breath. "Yep, you're right. Even better." I straighten the containers holding sugar, honey, and other coffee necessities. "I didn't know you were working today."

"I told Joanna I'd take the early shift. I've been here since six."

"Yuck."

"Right? I'll be off by one, though. Just in time for crafts and face painting."

I nod. "I, uh, have to tell you something."

She meets my eye and nods toward the door. "Okay. Join me on the porch while I straighten the furniture."

I slide off the stool and follow her out.

"What's up?" She rearranges the chairs under a wicker table. Before I can answer, she says, "Look who it is."

Kip emerges onto the porch, his muscles straining under the weight of the tools he carries. They must be done. He's packing up for the next job.

Olivia and I stand side by side. He glances up, grins, and winks. "Ladies."

We wave, mirrors of each other as he lumbers out to his truck. This time, I don't care that we look ridiculous.

Olivia's shoulder nudges mine. "Excited for your date tonight?"

"That's what I wanted to talk to you about."

She raises a brow.

"You're a good friend, Olivia. Thank you for helping me get what I wanted."

"Um, you're welcome?"

"The thing is—it's not what I want anymore. A lot has changed in the last two weeks. I can't date Kip. He's not even my type. Not really."

Her brow pulls together, and she opens her mouth. Closes it. Then she smiles. "You've fallen for your enemy, haven't you?"

I let out a breath. "Something like that."

She laughs. "Well, if I'm honest, Bryson's a better choice for you anyway."

"Why didn't you tell me that a long time ago?"

"I thought you hated him. And Kip was a fun distraction." She shrugs, but then her lips turn down. "Emma! Kip asked you out right in front of Bryson. And I pressured you to say yes. What did Bryson say after that?"

"I haven't talked to him."

She clamps her hands over her mouth, peeking at me with those bright hazel eyes. "I'm so sorry. I've messed everything up. I only wanted to help you. Maybe I can fix this."

"No!" I grab one of those hands and squeeze. "I've got this. And it's not your fault. I should've made amends with Bryson a long time ago."

"So what's your plan? Bryson knows you have a date with Kip."

"Well, for starters, I'm not going on that date." I nod toward Kip's truck. "I'm about to tell him I can't go. But I wanted you to know why. Do you think he'll be mad?"

He walks across the lawn and back into the house. "Nah. Something tells me there will be no shortage of dates for McDarcy."

"Maybe you should date him."

"Me? No. He's cute but not my type—at the moment."

Hmm. She's been spending a lot of time with Cole. "Do you happen to be into the cute, bossy, clipboard-carrying type—at the moment?"

She laughs and lifts a shoulder.

I'll take that as a yes.

***

Olivia was right. Kip didn't seem too bothered by our broken date. When I returned to Coffee Connection and relayed the conversation to her, he leaned against his truck, texting away. Making new evening plans, no doubt.

Now, with a bagel tucked in my bag, I head over to help set up the kids' craft area, taking photos as I go.

My boots crunch over fallen leaves as I pass the shiny Airstream food trucks. One is already open, serving chicken and waffles for breakfast. This area will be swarming by lunchtime.

Across Firefly Park, participants are warming up for the cornhole tournament. Their camaraderie is infectious as beanbags arc through the air—some hitting the mark and sinking into the hole while others flop wide and long into the grass.

The air hums and carries the sweet scent of candied pecans as I approach the pavilion and start setting up alongside the other volunteers. We spread mini pumpkins, googly eyes, glue, pipe cleaners, and glitter along the middle of the tables to be turned into a child's masterpiece.

All the while, my eyes scan the crowd for that shaggy light-brown hair.

At one o'clock, Olivia arrives, and we begin helping the kids decorate their pumpkins. Paint, plus glitter, plus preschoolers, what could go wrong?

After a while, paint covers every surface. Then a childish voice calls from across the space. "Emma!"

Tyler races across the pavilion. He's visited the face-painting booths.

He wedges himself between me and another kid. "I want to sit by you."

Mrs. Dumar, breathless as she tries to keep up, laughs. "Well, just make yourself at home, sweetie. Sorry, Emma."

"Oh, it's fine." I scoot over to pull in another chair. "Nice to see you, Spider-Man. I was hoping you would visit me."

His red, blue, and black painted cheeks bunch up into a smile. "It's me, Tyler!"

"Oh, right! I didn't recognize you. Hey, Tyler."

"Hi. Can I do a pumpkin?"

"Sure."

Mrs. Dumar ruffles his hair. "I'll be right over there when you're done." She points at a park bench where other women her age are chatting.

He nods and gets to work, reaching for the red and black paints. He's intent on keeping with the Spider-Man theme. Once I've helped him cover the pumpkin in sparkly red paint and he's begun to paint what must be a web, I prod for information. "I haven't seen Uncle Bryce today. Do you know where he is?"

He shrugs and dips a fresh paintbrush into the black paint. "He wasn't home when I woke up. Nana said he left."

What?

"Tyler, what do you mean he left? Where did he go?"

He shrugs again and then drops the paintbrush onto the plastic-covered table. "Owen!"

He abandons his work and rushes across the lawn to a kid about his age. Mrs. Dumar hurries to follow.

I begin tidying the space, but my gaze continues darting around the festival.

Did Bryson leave leave? As in leave town?

Surely not.

Or—is he avoiding me? I look at my watch. It's almost time to start the carnival games. We're scheduled to work the fishing game together. He wouldn't leave me to work alone, even if he were mad at me. He'll be there.

At quarter to three, I tromp over to our beautifully painted lake scene. He's not there, but maybe he's only running behind.

I set out the fishing poles, long sticks with a string attached. Each has a clip at the end where Bryson and I will clip a prize or piece of candy from behind the painted board.

I glance down the row of carnival games.

My hopes don't plummet until Cole wanders over with a girl I don't know.

He puts a hand out to introduce her. "Emma, this is Jade. She's filling in for Bryson."

"What? Where is he?" I catch my rudeness. "And hey, Jade. It's nice to meet you."

She smiles, and Cole adjusts his glasses. "I'm not sure where he is. He just said he couldn't make it. And he'd already found a replacement when he called me. Otherwise, I might've punched him for changing things at the last minute. Well, I've got to run. Have fun."

Bryson's avoiding me, for sure. I've botched everything. And it doesn't matter anyway. Bryson didn't care that I was to go out with Kip tonight. Why would he care that I'm not?

I paste on a smile. He's not ruining my afternoon. This will be fun, with or without McDoom. And besides, it's not Jade's fault. I beckon her over. "Come on. I'll show you what to do."

Hours later, as the afternoon sun begins its descent, the festive bubble I've forced myself to float around in starts to deflate. After the last kid reels in our last candy, we pack everything up.

I thank Jade for helping and shuffle toward home. The carnival goers wander down the hill toward hot dog stands and food trucks for dinner. I don't care to join them.

I pass the pavilion where the craft tables have been cleared away to make a dance floor. A band is setting up on the stage Kip built. They'll begin playing soon.

But I don't feel like dancing.

Why did I let my hopes get out of control? Bryson and I... there's too much history there. I've spent too much time hating him. He's spent too much time thinking I hate him. It was never going to work.

I point my feet toward Mema's, kicking at the leaves underfoot. I'm mentally preparing a cup of strong coffee and a long evening editing photos when my phone chimes with my Jane Austen quote of the day. I pull it from my pocket and swipe the words onto the screen.

Her heart did whisper that he had done it for her. ~ Pride and Prejudice *by Jane Austen*

Oh, Jane. What did he do besides cause trouble?

I tuck my phone away and turn onto Lower Greenway. But as I near the front yard, my pace slows.

My breath catches, and I glance around.

Who... did this?

My heart already knows.

29

Emma

I trace a finger along the shiny metal roof of the
perfect Little Free Library near Mema's front walk. The
pile of supplies I bought and my customized plans are
gone. It's an exact rendition of my design: a tiny porch,
a metal roof, and a big plexiglass door. The wood was
left natural, leaving me space to paint and add my own
splashes of color.

I turn, peering around the house. Is anyone watching,
waiting for me to find it? But everyone is at the festival.
The only sounds are the rustle of wind and the colorful
leaves fluttering across the pavement where long
shadows from the lowering sun have left their mark.

Kip would have never done this for me. Nor Audrey
or Olivia or any of my other friends. Certainly not

Mema. They've all been busy today. That leaves—
someone I haven't seen all day. Someone who told me
he took a woodworking class his sophomore year.
Someone who hasn't been my friend for a long time.

Bryson.

His house is still and quiet, and I start to step in that
direction when something catches my eye through the
plexiglass. I'd thought the library was empty, but two
lonely books are stacked on the bottom shelf.

I open the door and grab the one on top, a tattered
copy of Jane Austen's *Emma*. The corners of my mouth
lift as I run a hand over the cover... and my name.

My fingers brush a folded piece of paper tucked
between the pages, its edges slightly crumpled. I
swallow and unfold the note.

Emma,

I'm sorry I left you hanging today. Hopefully, this will
make up for it. You could've built the library yourself,
but I wanted to do it for you to say how very sorry I am
for everything. I had no idea how much trouble you got
into or how much trouble it caused you afterward. I
hope you'll forgive me.

I know you like Jane Austen, so I stopped by the used
books store in Eufaula today. Luckily, they had a few. I
like the name of this one, so it might be a good start to
your collection.

I hope you have fun on your date tonight. I truly
want you to be happy.

Please forgive me for ruining our friendship.

I've missed you.

Bryson

I smile, shaking my head, and wipe at the corners of my eyes. I can't believe he did this for me. And after I've been so terrible to him.

I turn toward his house, but my gaze lands on the other book.

I suck in a shallow breath. No.

I reach for it, and a small part of me—that thirteen-year-old self—writhes with embarrassment.

It's my first book, the one once filled with scribbles, snapshots, and the ramblings of a tween girl. I edited it years later and made it available for only a short time. The pages hold pieces of my soul no one besides my family and strangers have ever seen. It's not available for purchase anymore. I took it down when I published my first rom-com.

No. No. No.

Did Bryson *read* this?

I flip it open, and another sheet of paper flutters out. Oh no. I crumple it into my pocket and rush inside, not wanting anyone to witness my humiliation.

I wrote this book over the years while I was crushing on Bryson Dumar. I started it when I was twelve. It was meant to be a simple story about a girl and her sisters and their group of friends. It turned into a coming-of-age story about friendship, love, mistakes, and broken hearts.

What did Bryson think of this?

I flop onto the couch in the empty living room and pull the letter from my pocket. I smooth it over my knee and read.

Emma,

Please don't be mad, but I stayed up all night and read most of this book. I came away marveling over how clueless both of us were. It's far too late for us now, but I wanted you to know I really am sorry we never clicked. Three years ago, neither of us was observant enough to realize we liked each other. Or brave enough to put it out there. But that's okay. Time moves on.

What I would like now is for us to be friends again like we once were. Can we do that?

Again, I've missed you.

Bryson

I fold the paper and tuck it back into the book. He's right. We were so stupid. So clueless and afraid. But being fearful you might ruin a friendship with declarations of love is valid. Putting it out there is scary. Mixing love and friendship is complicated. But it might have been worth it. Might it still be?

Ruining a friendship because of stubbornness and an unwillingness to talk and forgive—that was the cowardly act in this narrative. He wasn't the antagonist of our story. I was. I'm the one who did something wrong. I broke the law by climbing that tower. Not him. And I punished him for trying to protect me.

I rush out the door and up Bryson's porch steps. The lights are off inside. I knock. No one answers.

Creeping around to the back of the house, I find his mom's car and his dad's truck in the driveway. He hasn't left Carlton Landing.

He must be at the festival, and there are things left to say.

***

But thirty minutes later, I stomp back into the house, up the stairs, and onto Mema's balcony. I still haven't found him.

In the distance, the band transitions into a fun, upbeat song, a severe contrast to my mood.

As the low sun casts a soft golden light over the balcony, I huff, grab a discarded blanket, and sink onto the love seat. I pull it tight around me, burying myself in my unanswered questions.

Bryson, where are you? And what will happen when I find you?

30

Bryson

I jolt awake, blinking the sleep from my eyes as the room swims into focus. Sunset is near, and shadows are starting to fill the space.

I fumble for my phone and then sit up. It's almost six thirty. Oh, man. I slept longer than I intended.

That happens when you stay up all night and into the next day.

Groaning, I roll out of bed and pad my way into the bathroom.

When I return, I sink onto the foot of my bed and run a hand through my hair.

Since it's already evening, I missed all the festival games, and the band started thirty minutes ago. I could go check it out.

I make a face. Emma will be there… with *him*.

No thanks.

But I can't let them keep me from hanging out with everyone. I have to get over it.

I'll get ready in fifteen minutes. Besides, I promised Tyler I'd take him on the hayride.

I peek out the curtains to the yard next door. Has Emma seen the library?

The street is empty. Quiet.

Pulling on a hoodie, I slide open the balcony door and step out into the chilly evening. The distant sound of the band drifts my way.

Emma's down there with her arms wrapped around Kip next to the stage he built with his own two hands.

Maybe I will stay home tonight.

I approach the railing, leaning over it, and let my gaze wander to the Little Free Library.

Putting it together was simple. She'd already bought almost everything, and I only had to make one trip to the hardware store this morning. Her plans were well-thought-out and based on some she found online. Easy.

I wander back to the hanging daybed and flop onto it, leaving one foot on the ground. It swings out and bumps the railing before settling into a smooth drift—back and forth.

Why did I sleep so long? I have no idea if she's seen what I did. And if she has, what did she think of it? A nervous jolt runs through my stomach.

And more importantly, will she be mad I read her book? The writing wasn't great, at least not as good as the one I read last week. She's learned a lot since that first novel, but I couldn't put it down. It was mostly about her, her sisters, and her family, but she'd included many stories about our childhood. How we met, the games we played, the adventures we shared, the hangouts we lazed through.

The almost kiss and exactly what was going on in her head as it almost happened.

I groan.

She'd wanted me to kiss her.

But I hadn't. I'd checked my text instead.

What an idiot.

After that, she assumed I wasn't interested, and the book veered into her broken heart, followed by her quick friendship with Eric. I stopped reading at this point. I knew I wouldn't make another appearance. I'd been cut out soon after. Besides, I had a library to build.

But now what?

The swing continues its lazy dance, an echo of the pendulum swinging in my chest. Stay or go, fight or flight, friends or enemies. I need to put an end to the chapter of my life entitled "Emma and the Endless What-Ifs."

All my friends are her friends. I can't avoid her—or Kip—here in this tiny place. Maybe I should visit my grandparents. Clear my head and then come back and be a better friend.

My heart needs to move on from Emma Kate Blackwell.

31

Emma

The crisp autumn air nips at my cheeks as I lay curled on the too-short love seat. I tug the blanket to cover my chin and nestle further into its warmth.

It's one of those perfect fall evenings where you can smell both leaves and a distant fireplace mingled together. The band kicks up their cover of an old but familiar country song. The sound tugs at the corners of my mouth. This kind of tune would have me tapping my feet if my heart wasn't lodged in my throat.

A creak from the balcony next door snatches my attention, and my breath catches when Bryson steps out into the soft glow of the setting sun.

I don't move, but my pulse jumps into overdrive.

Oblivious to my presence, he leans over and rests his elbows on the railing facing the street. He's lost in thought, or maybe he's simply enjoying the music.

He doesn't turn my way, though he probably wouldn't see me lying under this blanket, even if he did. I'm completely covered and stone still. He stares down at the library he built as his shoulders sink with a heavy sigh. An agitated hand rakes through his disheveled hair before he walks over to the hanging daybed, sinking onto it. It thumps against the wall.

I exhale a slow breath and swipe open my messaging app under the blanket. I begin a new text thread.

I deleted any old texts between us long ago, so there's no history to flip back through.

It feels like a fresh start—a new conversation.

I thumb out "hi" and hit send before I can overthink it.

The message floats through the digital ether to Bryson, who sits up so fast he bangs the daybed against the wall again.

I bite my lip and grin.

He steadies himself and stares at his phone, lips parted.

What's he thinking?

Tense seconds pass, and just when I assume he's decided to ignore my text, one comes through.

Bryson: hey

Well, it's a start. My turn. I spend way too long typing my next five words.

Me: I'm sorry I blocked you.

Bryson: it's ok

Me: it's not

Bryson: thanks for unblocking me

Me: thanks for the library

Bryson: you're welcome. I was wondering if you saw it.

Me: it's perfect

His lips turn up but flatten.
A typing bubble pops up, so I wait. It goes away, starts again, goes away again, and returns.

Bryson: how's your date going?

His knee starts to bounce.
I don't make him wait for my reply.

Me: I didn't go

His knee stops bouncing.

Bryson: oh

He's still for a few moments before sending his next text.

Bryson: why not?

Me: Lots of reasons

One of those being, I like you. A lot.

Me: He's pretty much a jerk.

Bryson: Finally. Something we can agree on. *Laughing emoji*

Grinning, I send the eye-roll emoji.

Bryson: Where are you?

Me: not far

His head is bent over his phone, brow drawn. I stand and quietly walk to the edge of Mema's balcony.

Me: can we start over?

Bryson: um… ok

He swats his hair out of his eye, and I grip the blanket tightly around my shoulders. The fabric is grounding—real—in a way the fluttering in my chest isn't.

Deep breath. "Hey, Brandon. What'cha doin'?"

His chin pops up, and a jolt runs through me when his gaze locks with mine across the empty space between our balconies. The corner of his mouth starts to turn up at my choice of words. He remembers when we had this conversation before. "Who's asking? And… it's Bryson."

"Right. It's me, Emma. I didn't know you were next door."

He stands and steps forward, mirroring my position, shoving his hands in his pocket. "I didn't know you were next door." He cocks his head to the side. "Have you been spying on me?"

"No."

"I'm pretty sure you were." He breaks away from the old conversation.

My lips stretch up as I hug the blanket closer. "Maybe."

We stare at each other until my gaze darts away to the floor. "I've been looking for you."

"Yeah? Sorry. I was sleeping. I sort of stayed up all night." He grips the railing, his gaze intent. "But… I've been here all along."

And he has. He's been here all along. Patiently waiting for me to wake up and do something about our lost friendship.

"I know. And I can't believe you did that." I dip my chin toward the library.

He lifts a shoulder. "I wanted to."

As if on cue, the band starts up a song we both know —a song from those carefree days when we were inseparable. It wraps around us like an old blanket, softening the edges of the present with memories of the past.

We both laugh, turning toward the band.

He shakes his head. "Remember this one?"

"Of course. We only listened to it a million times."

We listen, lost in memories, until I step closer, a hand on the railing. "You want to come over?"

"Yeah." He nods. "I'll be right there."

"It's open."

I return to the love seat, and butterflies swarm my stomach. There's more left to say, and I'll need to set aside my pride and say it.

A minute later, Bryson pushes through the balcony door, and my fingers tap an erratic rhythm on the armrest.

"Hey," he says.

"Hi." I still my fingers and slide a fall-themed pillow into my lap. "Can we talk?"

He nods and joins me on the love seat.

I turn my body toward him, unable to meet his eyes. "Bryson, I…" I pick at the corner of the pillow. "I'm sorry I was mad at you for so long. For letting our friendship just… disappear."

"Emma…"

I wave him off. "No, let me finish." I brave his gaze. "I blamed you, but… it was all me. You didn't do anything wrong. I climbed that tower. I shut you out. And… I'm so sorry." A tear rolls down my cheek.

He reaches up and thumbs the tear away. "Emma, I forgive you."

I tilt into his palm. "And… I've missed you too."

"Really?"

I smile. "Well, there may have been days when I didn't know it. But, yes."

His hand has moved to push my hair behind my ear. His voice is low. "So… friends?"

He's moved closer, or maybe it was me.

Friends? I suppose that's a good place to start. "Yes."

His thumb brushes along my jaw, and I reach out, taking his other hand.

He swallows and fits our fingers together. "And was I right? Is it too late for"—he meets my gaze—"us?"

I shake my head. "Definitely not."

He looks down at my lips, leaning closer.

His phone buzzes between us.

He stills. "You've got to be kidding."

I bite my lower lip to keep from laughing.

He grabs the phone and moves like he'll throw it off the balcony. Instead, he tosses it on a cushioned chair across from us. He's back in a flash, his hand back on my face, my fingers running through his hair.

We're both smiling in the last moments of the golden hour when his lips finally meet mine.

It's sweet and tentative, a question asked and answered all at once. It's the kind of kiss that speaks of second chances and of young love and old friendship. It feels like coming home.

"Uncle Bryce! Where are you?" A childish voice calls from inside their balcony door.

We break apart, breathless and laughing softly. Tyler steps out but doesn't see us as we stare at each other like a couple of lovesick fools. Which, really, I guess we are.

"Uncle Bry–*ice*!" Tyler calls again.

We laugh outright, and Tyler comes to his balcony's edge and plants his hands on his hips. "Where've you been? I thought we were going on the hayride. Nana texted."

"Sorry, buddy. I was… napping."

"You're not napping." His eyebrows squinch together. "What are you guys doing out here?"

"Talking."

"About what?"

"Just stuff. Friendship."

"Oh, about how friendship with girls is complicated?"

I raise a brow, and Bryson chuckles. "Yep. Exactly."

"Well, are you friends?"

Bryson and I look at each other. He answers first. "I think so. Right, Emma?"

"For sure."

Tyler wipes glitter from his hands onto his jeans. "Just friends?"

Bryson glances my way. "Uh."

I snicker, but Tyler's already moving on. "So, can you take me on the hayride?"

"Can Nana take you?"

"But you promised," Tyler whines.

I bump Bryson's shoulder. "I mean, if you promised…"

He kisses my nose. "Okay, buddy. I'll meet you outside."

"Yeah!" He fist pumps the air and runs to the door. "Bring Emma."

In one smooth motion, Bryson stands, pulling me with him. We're face-to-face as he runs a hand down my forearm.

"Want to join us?"

I step closer, threading our fingers together. "Sure. Just friends?"

Bryson puts another kiss on my lips before tugging me toward the door. "Definitely not."

32

Emma

"Emma, come try this," Olivia says as I type away on
my laptop at my usual window table.

"Give me a sec."

She starts the espresso machine on one last coffee,
and the aroma in the shop intensifies. "It's almost
closing time too. You better pack it up."

"Okay, I'm almost done."

And I really am. This story has poured out of me over
the last month. I already had most of it planned and
even some written, but then, everything came together.
I've stayed up into the wee hours every morning—after
hanging out with Bryson, of course. I even cut back on
my hours at the coffee shop to get this done. I might not
have any extra spending money, but I found my muse.

My lips turn up as I finally, finally type out that last sentence and then add the words *The End* to the bottom.

I sit back and release a quiet laugh. I did it. This is only a first draft, so there's a ton of work left to do, but this phase is complete.

Still smiling, I gaze out the window. The house next door is almost done. The carpenters are gone, and other crews who perform different jobs have been in and out. Soon, a family will move in and start making their own Carlton Landing memories. I've hardly thought of Kip, and I have no doubt he hasn't thought of me.

And that's totally fine.

I did get my inspiration after all. It turns out I had that meet-cute near Firefly Park seven years ago.

I close my laptop and skip over to the coffee bar. "First draft. Done."

Olivia is pouring steamed milk into a mug. "You finished?"

"Yep."

"Yay! Congratulations."

"Thank you."

She sets the mug in front of me. "Okay, let's celebrate by trying my new drink."

I pull it close. "Mmm. It smells good. Cinnamon, right?"

"Yeah. I call it a cinnamon cookie latte."

I test a sip. "Oh wow. That's great. But what about your famous gingerbread lattes?"

"Oh, don't worry. I'm already selling tons of those."

I take another sip. "Everyone will love this. Has Joanna tried it?"

Olivia nods toward the chalkboard next to the coffee bar. "She approved it for the menu this morning." She rests her elbows on the bar across from me and laces her fingers together. "Pretty please, can you put it on there? You're so much better at it than me."

I laugh and then savor another sip. "You don't have to beg. I love doing the chalkboard. Hand over the chalk."

Minutes later, I step back to admire the plate of cookies, mug, saucer, and Christmas tree I've drawn beneath the words *Try our all-new Cinnamon Cookie Latte.*

I hold it up for Olivia to see. "Perfect. Thank you. And I have a surprise for you. You're the only person in the world I would do this for."

I set the sign down, and she reaches under the counter and retrieves a new copy of *Pride and Prejudice.* She places it in front of me. "I'm already a quarter of the way through."

I clap my hands. "Are you serious? You're reading it?" I hug the pages to my chest and then run a hand over the cover. "This is the best gift you've ever gotten me."

She rolls her eyes. "I've never gotten you a gift before." She snatches it back. "And you can't have it until I'm done. But when I am, you can put it in your library."

"Thank you, Olivia. And then we can watch the movie together."

"Yeah, yeah. We'll see if I like it first."

"Oh, you will."

My phone buzzes in my pocket, and I slide free. "Oh! Speaking of, look who it is." I turn my phone to her. "The Jane Austen Daily."

She squints and reads it aloud.

"'The person, be it gentleman or lady, who has not pleasure in a good novel, must be intolerably stupid.'" She scrunches her nose. "Um, that's a bit unsettling. Did you plan that?"

I chuckle at the timely *Northanger Abbey* quote. "Nope."

"Hmm. Well, challenge accepted, Jane." She pitches her voice toward my phone. "Guess I better enjoy it."

"Like I said, you will."

She starts cleaning the espresso machine. "How's the library going?"

"It's great. Everyone seems to love it. Several people come by every day. And the kids on bikes have already cleaned out the kids' section. I need to find more children's books."

I painted it light gray with blue and yellow accents to match Mema's house. I even hung mini battery-powered twinkle lights on the porch for Christmastime.

Olivia straightens her over-the-top holiday earrings. "Maybe I should try an Emmie Blackwell book next."

I rest against the counter. "Maybe you should."

The last customer leaves with a ding, and I help Olivia close the register and wipe the tables.

I'm stacking plates behind the counter when the door dings again, and I turn toward it. "We're clos—"

But I cut off as a grin stretches across my face.

I can't help it. Not when Bryson Dumar enters a room.

The last few weeks have been the best. Bryson and I have spent time catching up on everything we missed over the last three years. We've also kayaked, gone on dinner dates to Eufaula, watched movies with our friends, and even volunteered to help Cole with upcoming Christmas festivities.

Not to mention, I'm passing my very last high school class. I should have my diploma in a matter of weeks.

Olivia moves to stand next to me. "Oh, look, it's McDoom." She smiles good-naturedly, and I elbow her. "Don't call him that."

She places a hand on her chest. "What? I'm pretty sure I learned that from you. Right, Bryson?"

He sits on a stool and props his elbows on the coffee bar, angling toward me. "You know, I do think she has her facts straight."

"Ha ha." I shake my head. "As you know, I've had a change of heart."

I reach across the space and thread my fingers through his.

Olivia backs away. "Oh, I noticed."

"What are you doing here?" I ask.

"Well… I was playing a super-manly board game with my sister and Tyler."

Olivia puts up a hand. "Let me guess. You want a coffee after closing time?"

"Actually, I was hoping just that." He plants a sheepish grin on his face and slaps a five-dollar bill onto the counter. "Run it in the morning?"

Olivia slips the bill in front of the register. "Okay, but your *girlfriend* has to make it this time. I need to straighten the supply room."

She saunters down the hall, and Bryson squeezes my fingers. "Girlfriend. I'm still not used to hearing that."

"Well, it was seven years in the making."

"True enough."

"Don't tell me you lost at Candy Land again?"

"Uh—Maybe."

I grab his hand and haul him toward my table. "I'll teach you how to make a pour-over, but first, I have to show you something."

I flip open my laptop and point to the words *The End*.

"You did it! I knew you could. Is it ready for the editor?"

"Oh no. Not a chance. But the first draft is done."

He pulls me in for a hug, resting his chin on my head. "Way to go. One step closer."

I ease away, but only slightly, and stare into those dark eyes I love so much. "And another thing."

"Yeah?"

I let my gaze slide up to the ceiling. A bundle of mistletoe hangs above our heads. Once he follows my gaze and laughs, I step closer. "I would hate to miss this opportunity."

"Yes, that would be a shame."

He leans down, and we're both smiling when he presses his lips to mine.

The End

What to read next?

If you haven't already, read Morgan and Will's Carlton Landing love story in *My Favorite Color is Your Something Blue*! These books can be read in any order. Read a synopsis: www.evaaustin.com/ysb-synopsis/

Want to get more sweet YA romance book suggestions? Sign up, and I'll send your first recommendation now! Visit: www.evaaustin.com/signup/

Dear Reader,

Thank you so much for reading this teen and young adult romance! It means so much that you gave *My Favorite Color is The Golden Hour* a chance.

Are you looking for more sweet romance books like this one? Me too! I'm always searching for books to suggest to my readers. Sign up for my newsletter, and I'll send book recommendations as I find them. (I'll also let you know when the next *Favorite Color* book comes out!) Visit evaaustin.com/signup/, and don't forget to follow me on Instagram.

If you have questions about this book, the next in the series, or writing, please email via the contact form on my website. I look forward to hearing from you!

- Eva

Acknowledgments

I want to thank my wonderful family for supporting me in my writing journey! Thanks to my husband for being my biggest encourager. You're the one who consistently asked, "What's your next goal?" or "Did you meet your goal today?" Thanks for keeping me accountable!

Thank you also to my kids for encouraging me and putting up with writing weekends and holiday editing. I love you so much and can't wait to see what God has in store for you!

And a special thanks to my editor, Deirdre. You tell it like it is, and I love it!

Eva Austin is a fiction writer, author of contemporary novels for teens who want to be swept away in a fun, light-hearted, sweet love story.

Eva holds a BS from the journalism and mass communication department of Abilene Christian University. She teaches digital art to high school students while also managing her blog, Book Series Recaps, and writing fantasy stories under the name Sara Watterson.

When not writing, teaching, or enjoying her kids' many activities, Eva likes reading on the back porch, drinking coffee, and hanging out with her super-cute hubby. She lives in central Oklahoma with her husband and three children.

Stay up to date by joining Eva's mailing list here:
https://www.evaaustin.com

Let's be friends:
https://www.instagram.com/eva.austin.author
https://www.goodreads.com/eva_austin

Made in the USA
Las Vegas, NV
30 November 2024

12930344R00152